I0652955

LA MÁQUINA OSCURA

D.G. SUTTER

Westphalia Press
An imprint of the Policy Studies Organization

Also from Westphalia Press

westphaliapress.org

LA MÁQUINA OSCURA

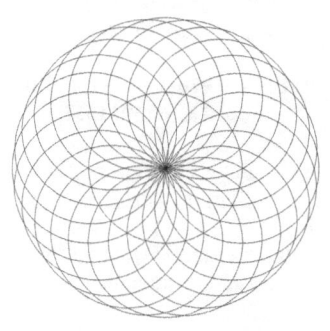

La Máquina Oscura
by D. G. Sutter
All Rights Reserved © 2015 by Policy Studies Organization

Westphalia Press
An imprint of Policy Studies Organization
1527 New Hampshire Ave., NW
Washington, D.C. 20036
info@ipsonet.org

ISBN-13: 978-1-63391-155-0
ISBN-10:1633911551

Cover and Interior design by Taillefer Long at Illuminated Stories:
www.illuminatedstories.com

Daniel Gutierrez-Sandoval, Executive Director
PSO and Westphalia Press

Rahima Schwenkbeck, Director of Media and Marketing
PSO and Westphalia Press

Updated material and comments on this edition
can be found at the Westphalia Press website:

www.westphaliapress.org

For Brenna,
Your faith in this book never wavered and, for that,
I am grateful. I love you.

CONTENTS

"Vanished like fire or air, an element of the earth back into the earth. To mix with the everyone-else people that never ceased to be. Poured out among them. The evaporated girl, he thought. Of transformation. That comes and goes as she will. And no one, nothing, can hold on to her."

-Phillip K. Dick, *A Scanner Darkly*

Chapter 1

THE SHIFT

The sun permeated the flat rock of Marco's abdomen, darkening the hue of his skin to cobalt brown, as he lay on the reclining mesh beach chair. The heat was intense, the sort that made the corners of his eyes curl up at the ends, floating waves forcing him to squint, blurring his vision. They whirled in the sky like run-off from burnt gasoline, weaving translucent images over the deep blue sky. Marco wore expensive shades, Ray-Ban or Fossil, something designer. It didn't make a difference, as his eyes were closed beneath the three-hundred dollar pair.

Sheila, his wife, relaxed on his right—her half-Irish, half-German skin turning pink under the cruel hand of the sunbeams. She was washed in a concoction of sunscreen and baby oil, making her skin gleam. The screen was to protect from a burn, the oil to induce a tan—a bit of a contradiction. They were far enough from the ocean to remain dry, yet close enough to feel the fan-like breeze, salty and pure.

A ball landed in the sand next to Marco's chair and he woke with a start. He noticed the intrusive object and kicked it to the young boy with his foot.

"Lo siento!" the kid apologized, grabbing the rubber sphere.

Marco stretched his toes toward the ocean where pontoons and sailboats bobbed above the weeds and creatures of the deep. He dreamed of the turtles below the surface, staring at the manmade devices—unidentified sailing objects—and wondering what-in-the-hell they were with their bulging eyes.

Marco yawned and held his head up with his hand. How good it felt to be back in the home country of Spain, how years seemed like millennia, and he wondered why his parents had ever immigrated to America. His mother was still living there, alone. He often thought of her, rather fretted for her. Yet, she always reassured him over the distant stretch of telephone wire that she was just fine. Marco took a deep breath. Worry was never eased.

He closed his eyes once more and must have drifted off for a few moments, for when he opened his eyes again the sun was dipping below the horizon and the beach-goers were starting to pack in.

"You almost ready?" he asked his wife.

Sheila flinched at Marco's mental invasion and the sunglasses nearly fell from her beautifully thin face.

He felt a wee bit of guilt at waking her, but was unaware of the fact that she was off in dreamland.

"What?"

"Are you almost ready to head back to the hotel? Dinner reservations are at six, you know."

Sheila sat up quickly and pulled the straps of her bikini tightly to-gether in an angry knot. She forged a ponytail with her locks of brown hair, bonding it together with elastic.

"Shit," she said. "What time is it?"

Marco dug into his backpack and found the pocket watch, which Sheila had given him, in the rear zipper compartment. "Four twenty-two."

Sheila shifted uncomfortably, as if the chair was touching her in places that she didn't deem appropriate. "Damn it, Marco! I've been sleeping for two hours? You couldn't have woken me up?"

She started tossing belongings into her green and blue beach bag. "I'm going to be so fucking burnt." She wrapped a towel over her shoulders and pulled it taut, shaking in that too-much-sun shiver.

She acted like it was his fault, like he had purposefully let her sleep so that she would incur a burn. The weird thing was that Marco couldn't remember falling asleep. One minute he'd been contemplating the Costa da Morte (or the Coast of Death, as it is known), the next he was contemplating his eyelids.

No, he blamed the sun. Obviously, the sun had a pact with the Sandman. In exchange for the sleeping humans, the Sandman pays with unloaded and unabashed rays. There was no way around sleep for Marco on a long day in the sun. It came naturally. The warmth put a spell over his mind, making him fuzzy and worn-out inside.

He sat up, again yawning. It was exceptionally bright for being past four o'clock, not like the sun to stay up so late. Marco folded his beach chair, gently shook it free of sand, and then slid on his sandals. He noticed that Sheila was already halfway up the beach.

As he started to walk, the ground gave a slight shake. It was more of a tremor, like when you're on the third floor of a shopping mall and it feels as though the building will collapse upon itself, rather than an actual shift in tectonics. Yet, it was there. Marco pictured the giant plates sliding over each other miles beneath the ground, slithering like giant slugs and provoking a deep fear within the man, his fear of natural disaster. It happened again and Marco planted his feet shoulder-width in a useless brace.

Sheila glanced over her shoulder, her eyes wrinkled at the edges. She was tensed and prepared to run to Marco, yet was apparently frozen in her sandals. Marco knew she was looking for his support across the distance. He mouthed "It's okay."

The ground shook once more and then all was still. Quite a few of the landlubbers had grabbed their things and fled for more solid ground. The yells and cries were blocked from Marco's ears by way of personal defense. Some looked around frantically, Marco assumed for loved ones. He jogged up to his.

She looked terrified, and horrifically burnt. "Marco, what was that?"

"That felt like the beginning of an earthquake," Sheila said, shaking her head on the verge of breakdown. "No, I don't want there to be an earthquake."

Marco couldn't help but laugh sarcastically. It was a little bit of out of their control. "I'm afraid there's not much you could do to prevent it," he said with a chuckle.

"I'm scared. What if there is one?"

"Then there is. The first step is to get the hell away from the water. An earthquake can cause a tsunami." He grabbed her hand and they hurried over the beach road covered in sand, which led to their hotel.

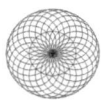

Marco tipped the hotel service guy five bucks for bringing fresh towels. The gentleman looked displeased, but Marco didn't care. He was lucky to get anything at all. It always bothered Marco how service-people receive tips for doing their job. They made out like bandits, probably made more than he did in a month!

The only service-people in his mind worthy of tips were waitresses, given their shitty wages. Marco worked in a cafe and Sheila—coincidentally—a waitress at a high-end steak shop in Madrid, but they scraped by. They needed very little to stay happy, and had no dependents except for each other.

If Marco was about, one could bet Sheila was at his side or just around the corner. They were together most of the time. Though, some would claim it a poisonous relation (spending the amount of time with one another they did), both of them liked it that way. Other people clogged up your life unnecessarily—especially, the conditionals. If you had your family and your lover, then what else is needed in life?

Marco dropped one of the clean, white towels on the sink, which was wet from the perspiration of her long wash, and hung the other on the towel rack. He closed the door slowly, trying to avoid a breeze chilling her exit. Nothing worse than stepping out of a hot shower and into cold air, thought Marco.

He sat on the edge of the queen-sized bed. Sheila had a habit of tearing the comforter off the bed at hotels and sleeping with the sheets. She was terrified of bed bugs and those tall tales claiming the comforters are never cleaned, and you wake up with a semen stain in front of your eyes. The reason he let her do it was because he believed her. Though he would never let on to her superstition—that would be too easy.

Marco lay back on the bed and flipped on the tube. Earlier the newsman had claimed the shaking as a simple tremor—nothing more, nothing less. Growing up in Southern California Marco had endured innumerable earthquakes. Plain and simple, to Marco it hadn't felt like one. However, not letting Sheila on to certain things helped on occasion. He didn't want to alarm Sheila from Pough-keepsie—sheltered Sheila as Marco sometimes humored himself. She had an allowance until age eighteen and then moved in with him, never forced to brave adulthood on her own.

There was nothing on the boob tube, but novelas. His mother had always watched them on the Spanish channels. He hated novelas. Marco clicked the television off and rested his hands underneath his head. The tide was rolling in, wetting dry sand and shoving crustaceans onto the shore. He could see a crab waddling along the water line. Then, a seagull dipped and scooped it up in its beak, reminding him of the benefits of being a larger creature.

The shower shut off and the curtain drew squeakily across the bar. The waves splashed soundlessly on the beach, but Marco wanted to hear them. He stood and slid the glass door away, stepping onto the balcony and closing his eyes, allowing the beauty to wash into his ears like a conch shell. The sound was what always got him, more so than the view. It soothed and transported you away, on a sail across the world, to any destination of your desire.

Sheila broke his daydream in half with her commanding voice. "Can you close that door? That breeze is goddamn freezing!"

Chapter 2

A CALL FOR HELP

Dinner was amazing. Marco had gotten Paella spiced lightly with Spanish paprika, or pimenton. It was a dish his mother used to make for the neighborhood, purely Spanish comfort food, hard to find it made correctly in America. Being back on the home front, it was so easy to indulge. He didn't have to wait for his mother to make the meal—or for Sheila to fail miserably at attempting it. Traditional dishes are best left to those fed and bred upon them, thought Marco.

They had been living in Montejo de la Sierra—a small village in the province of Madrid—for three months when they decided to take a summer vacation on the Costa da Morte. The coast is known for the numerous shipwrecks that frequently occur there, more modernly the 2002 shipwreck of the Prestige oil tanker. The jagged cliffs love to grab hold of ships and send them crashing to the bottom of the cold sea. Marco felt for the fishermen in Spain who had lost profit (his uncle being one of them), and also for the suffering sea life.

He and Sheila stayed not far from a strip of land named Finisterre, sometimes referred to as the coast of death. Marco wondered why anyone would want to stay at a place with such a reputation on vacation, or live there for that matter. The name alone was a deterrent.

He had opted for the Eastern shore, near Barcelona or Valencia, while Sheila had pushed for the Northwest coast. He realized it was her love for solitude. She enjoyed places where there were little to no people. Overcrowded beaches were to be avoided at all costs. The place was rich with wild, deprived of tourists, and is one of the most untouched lands in the country, home to many relics and treasures, including some of the most well-preserved cave paintings known to man. Sheila had a love for old things, a love for things scenic, and a love for life. Beyond a shadow of a doubt, she was the worldliest woman Marco had ever met.

It was one of the many traits of hers that he adored, despite the pushiness—that was an acquired gene. Her mother was constantly on her ass about things she should do in life and in her career. There was absolutely no sound decision Sheila could make without being scrutinized. Every choice she made happened to come under the microscope. Given all folks are capable of critiquing, Jennifer's were rarely positive, and that included Marco. She'd been telling Sheila to leave him ever since the beginning, claiming he had no direction. He begged to differ. They were aimed in exactly the right direction—for a slow-paced life in a laid-back country.

Once the pressure of moving and Sheila's mother was gone, they needed an escape. Thus, they spent the week on the Costa da Morte. There was time enough to hop in and visit Marco's uncle, Ricky, who lived near Finisterre. They spent an afternoon at his small house on the hill, eating tapas and drinking wine. It was a shame when they had to pack in and leave. He rarely saw his uncle and Marco could relax all day, every day, with family, eating fine food and drinking, for as the motto of Spain goes: "Eat when you drink, drink when you eat."

After his uncle's house, they'd checked into the hotel. He missed it already and was not prepared for the eight-hour drive back to Madrid. Driving on the left side of the road was something with which he was still unaccustomed, and it often led to an oncoming driver laying on the horn. It didn't help that Marco had a tendency of falling asleep at the wheel. Pedestrians, animals, and motorists alike became potential prey.

Along the Autovia del Noroeste, the highway heading South from Finisterre, Sheila fell asleep, snoring like a pig. Marco flipped the radio dial to light classical, something he only enjoyed listening to when he drove. A piano scaled up and down the eighty-eight keys—quietly, barely there, discreet. At times the sort of music could be so beautiful, so atmospheric, but it needed to be in the correct moment.

The sky was purple and the ocean smashed against the coast, tearing off pieces of the cliff. A woman was standing with her back to Marco, hitting herself in the head with a stone. Then, she grew frantic, whipping her arms about and tearing strands of hair from their follicles. The woman ran and jumped from the cliff, plummeting toward the loosely clumped boulders adorning the seashore. Before she could hit Marco's eyes clammed open.

The car was centered in the right lane—for once—thank God.

The image in the dream was gruesome. The woman who jumped off of the cliff reminded Marco of his mother. She was short and plump with graying hair. For some reason the dream urged him to pull over, find a phone, and dial her. He couldn't say why.

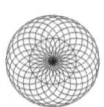

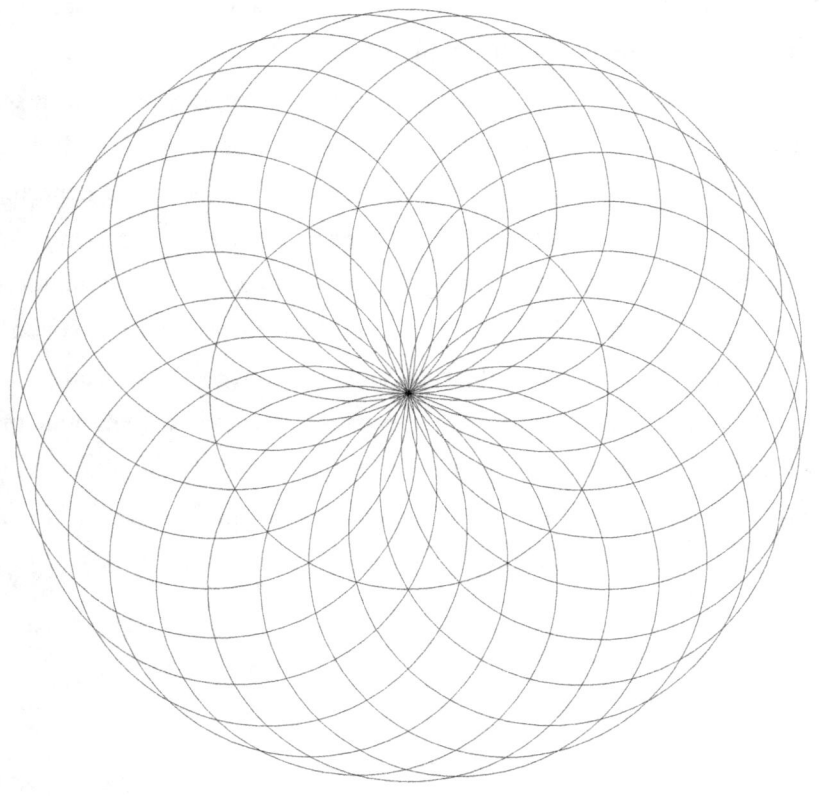

Chapter 3

SACRED GROUND

The three boys were adventuring as boys typically do on summer break. Their skin was turning dark brown from the unrelenting sun that was beating down on the mountainside. Time spent outdoors was never wasted for Ernesto, Juan, or Christian. They spent hours and hours in the forest of El Chapparal—tossing rocks, playing hide-and-seek, and climbing trees. Surely, one of them was late for lunch each day.

"Vamanos! Vamanos!" Ernesto chanted while running.

He was always the leader of the group, the one whom the others looked at for guidance, though the trio was as thick as thieves. While they played near the well at the foot of the mountain, the ground began to shake beneath their curious toes and Juan curled into a ball on the ground, covering his neck.

"*Christian!*" Juan yelled for his sibling. The older brother rushed to him, assuring that everything would be just fine.

As Juan slowly calmed and struggled to stand, Ernesto noticed the massive thing jutting from the mountain peak, round and copper like a rusted can of black beans.

He pointed toward the summit and patted Christian on the back. "Mira!"

Juan and Christian both gazed up the side of the slope to where the ground was crumbling away, boulders tumbling into the thicket of trees, and a sick rumbling was washing the slope. The ground shook two subsequent times and the boys exchanged frightened stares. Though scared, Ernesto was desperate to view the surfacing culprit. He coaxed the boys into following, but knew they would need to avoid park rangers, for it was unlawful to travel the forest without a permit or accompaniment.

When they were close enough to scrutinize, Ernesto thought it looked more like a large metal cake—subtract the delicious, fluffy frosting—than a can. He thought maybe, just maybe, it was a birthday wish for somebody—but whom?

He jumped onto the metal obstruction with a solid *"Tink!"* The engravings along the top rim were set deep, the corners of the ancient symbols filled with earthen clay. Christian told Ernesto to climb down, but he didn't listen. He was a boy with his own determination and brushed at one of the symbols, which was similar to a light switch. He kicked it. Beneath his feet was a long initiation of metallic grinding and cranking clicks. The machine slowly began to rotate and rise free of the soil.

"¡Baja de ahi!" Christian warned. *Get down from there!*

Ernesto laughed as the contraption spun like a carousel, but when it picked up speed, Ernesto no longer felt playful. His heart skipped, his feet started to lose their traction.

Christian again pleaded for him to jump off the machine, but it had started to spin out of control. The other boys backed off warily, unsure of the nature of the machine. They were caught between running for help and sticking around to see the consequence of Ernesto's action.

He started to stumble like a dizzy mouse. The landscape passed in a whirl, becoming a furthermore disturbed replication of a Van Gogh painting.

Juan and Christian finally decided to run for help, but forgetting the golden rule of the buddy system, left Ernesto to spin unaccompanied. He began to weep a long, wet sorrowful cry. His tears flung across the mountainside like rain, and he prayed that his mother would save him, begged for the hand of God.

Ernesto could see the forms of his friends diminishing down the mountain, until all at once he was alone. The machine showed no sign of stopping—let alone slowing—and Ernesto gave in, collapsing on top of the atrocity. His vomit spilled onto the disc, his face resting in the chunky excretion.

The machine picked up more speed, pulling him to the edge by the sheer will of gravity, and flung him from its circumference. His discarded body bounced across the rocky terrain, coming to rest some twenty feet from the protrusion. The rag doll bled from his head after colliding with a boulder, like a stray tennis ball cracked at the seams and leaking onto the sacred ground.

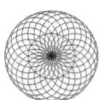

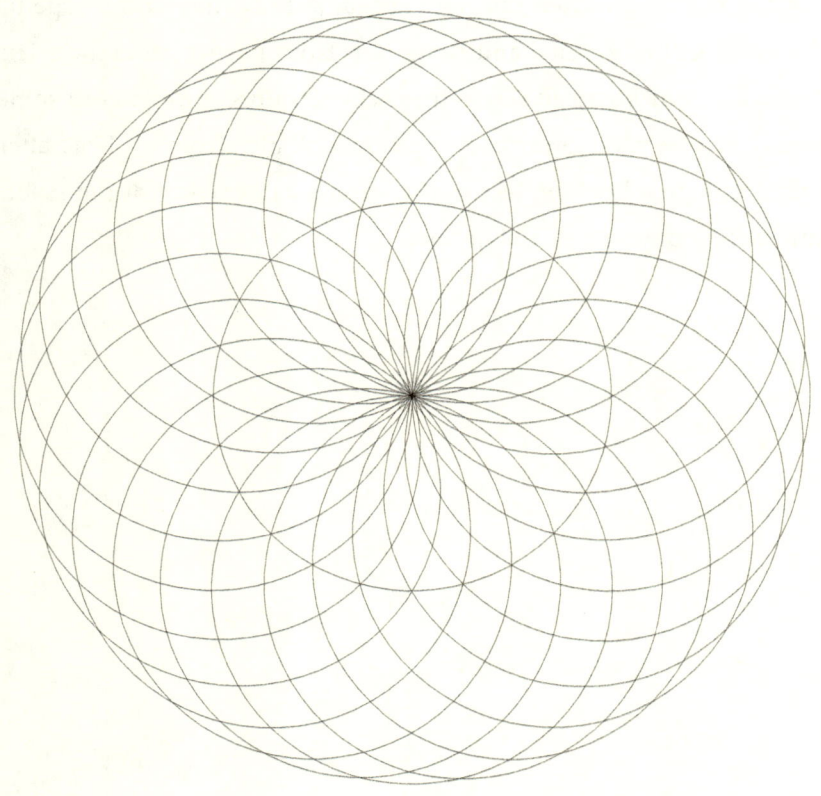

Chapter 4

SELF-PRESERVATION

Sal tossed the empty Butterfinger wrapper out of the car window, tainted with leftover chocolate. His Porsche Nine Eleven roared down Interstate 10, as the wrapper floated like a piece of shit across the highway. He used his fat finger to switch on KZE FM radio, through an initial snow of radio waves.

"…traffic's getting heavy down Ten East. If you're heading toward Los Angeles I would switch routes. There's an accident right at the mouth of Three-B, getting heavier by the minute. This is your traffic navigator Andy 'Hawkeye' Smithson, signing off… on K-Z-E, L.A.'s classic rock."

Sal spun the wheel to the right and got off at exit two. There was no way he was going to wade through all that traffic. A car flew by, passing on the left and almost sideswiping him, and he yelled *"Hey Asshole!"* out the window. He lifted his hand in a "What gives?" gesture.

Sal sped up to try and catch him, but the other driver had a lead foot. He was going to give him the bird, make a statement. Assholes with no penchant for other drivers, he thought.

He turned the car down Pacific Avenue. However, at the intersection to Windward, the traffic was backed up.

"Son-of-a-bitch!" He slammed his fist on the horn. Sal had never seen it so congested. Sometimes you get the slow drivers, rubbernecking to check out the freaks, but never to a complete standstill. He craned his neck out the window in curiosity, air conditioning leaking from the open passage, rising to assist with the deterioration of the ozone layer.

Twenty cars back and he could still see the traffic light. All three colors were blinking in rapid succession. Yet, another unseen marvel. Drivers honked to imply their aggravation and bicyclists weaved throughout the labyrinth of metal. Where there should have been a traffic director was a conglomeration of idling vehicles, all vying for the right-of-way.

A jackass in a black convertible Saab opened up to pass on the left and T-boned a red Toyota. The Camry spun into the cars parked at the stoplight behind it, causing a four car pile-up. On the sidewalk pedestrians shed their Venice boardwalk shenanigans to get in on the action. Camera phones started to come out of pockets and faces mocked concern.

The driver of the convertible stumbled from his car, screaming about how it was the poor woman's fault. She stepped out of her car crying and bleeding from the forehead. Sal laughed and rested his sweaty forehead in his palm. He could tell it was going to be a long day for Sal Pergotti. What other obstructions, he wondered.

Then, alarmingly, the ground started to shake. Quick as mice, folks left their cars behind. Eager to abandon the technology they so dearly relied upon. They dove into doorframes and sprinted away from buildings altogether. Sal wondered if they would do the same for their houses.

In the middle of the intersection, the pavement started to crack. If it had been any hotter, Sal would have thought it was a heat bubble. Suddenly pieces of the road started to crumble away like stale bread. The area cleaned out even more; most of the onlookers started running down the block.

Worst of all, the man from the convertible was perched atop the oddity. It was much like a large metal cake with a rusted bronze frosting. Slowly, it cracked from the shell of the Earth—a spinning jackhammer.

The man standing on top was screaming and the little old lady scrambled back to her Camry. Her car rumbled to a start.

More cars honked nervously and tried to escape. The streets were utterly congested, but people were desperate to get away. The street became a giant snake of mechanical evasion.

The object at the epicenter of the bisecting roads sped up and the man panicked. His attempted vault from the obscure machine landed him amongst the rubble, which had once belonged to a complete Boulevard. One of his legs caught between the ground and the bottom of machine, and the perpetrator of the accident was spun three hundred and sixty degrees.

His jeans snagged onto something Sal couldn't see and his body was thrown against the convertible. Left behind was the leg, which had been caught within the Earth. His blood painted the circumference of the thing. He would have been screaming in anguish had he not hit his head on the door of the car, knocking him unconscious.

Sal reversed, hit someone's fender, disregarded, and pulled onto the sidewalk. Folks were fleeing in all directions, but Sal was only consumed with his own well-being. Despite his civilian duty to the man who had lost a limb, he tore ass over the pedestrians' walkway.

He didn't slow until he reached Route 90 and then was able to pull back onto Interstate 405. The body he had clipped driving on the sidewalk barely slowed his progress. He could feel stronger forces at work, far larger and more important than humanity, and he didn't want to mess with them.

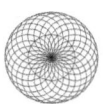

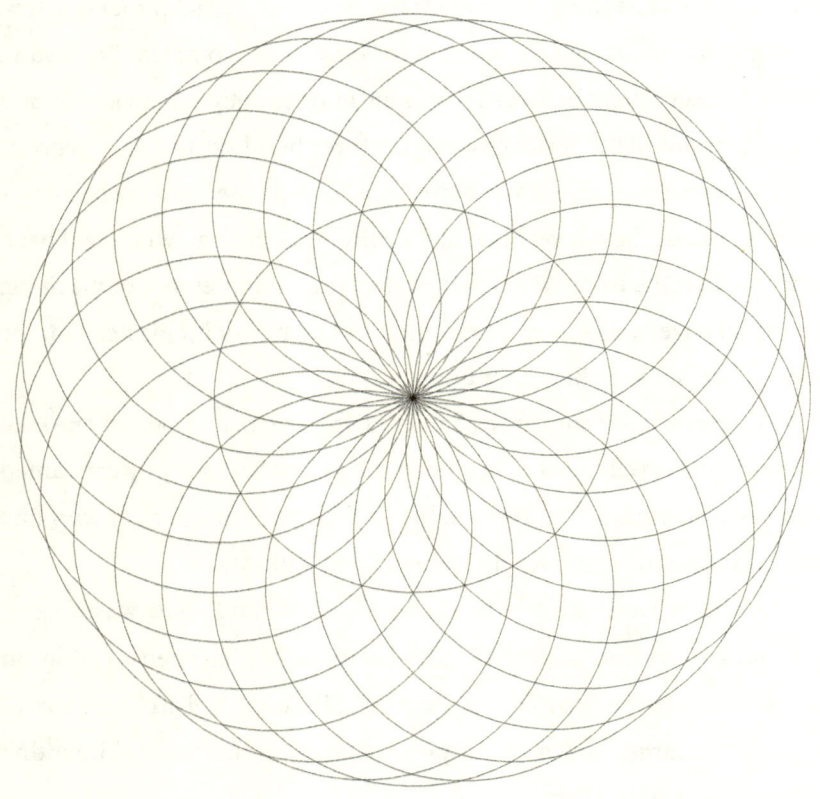

Chapter 5

BACK IN THE GROUND

They drove the remainder of the return trip with the radio off. Marco had left his window open, wind whipping his face as he drove. He didn't fall asleep, but attributed that to the two twenty-four ounce coffees he'd drank.

When they pulled into Montejo de la Sierra, a funeral was in procession. Marco hoped it wasn't Manuel's, his boss at the cafe. Manuel had been struggling trying to stay healthy of late. His cholesterol levels were high and his knee was becoming a bother. Marco tried to warn him against eating cream cheese, but Manuel was too stubborn. It was his only addiction—a bagel with the stuff on it, every morning. On top of it all he also had an exceptional case of asthma, which was easily triggered by heat or dust.

Marco was relieved to see Manuel's bald spot. He stood with his back to the passing car, the bald spot indicating his good health, at least for the time being. Being such a small village, however, Marco would know the identity of the deceased.

The priest dipped and tossed his arms about, throwing holy water on the coffin. Manuel glanced over his shoulder at the car. He gave a somber nod, and then respectfully returned to the funeral. Behind Manuel was Ernesto's mother, Angelica, leaning over the coffin and sobbing. Marco swallowed hard, knowing full well for whom the single mother's tears fell.

Sheila must have put the pieces together, too, for she gasped and started to cry lightly. Marco could feel his mouth become a frown—the poor boy. He was a good kid, always staying out of trouble. Sometimes Marco would play soccer with him out in the field in the foothills. Ernesto wanted to be "just like Ronaldo" when he grew up. Now the boy was in a casket, suddenly a box of bones.

Marco pulled over and parked. They held hands and walked closer to the crowd, stood next to Manuel on the outskirts. Manuel squeezed Marco's shoulder. It was an apologetic gesture. Ernesto's father was absent (run off when he was a baby) and for the past three months Marco had grown close to the boy, becoming a semblance of a big brother. He wished he could shed a tear for the boy, instead he sent a prayer.

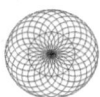

Marco drank the glass of water, chugging it as if it was the finest water from the purest well in the world. Droplets landed in his black goatee and stained his white t-shirt. The Montejos del Rincon mountain range stood stoically beyond the town limits. Manuel had told him of the machine, which had risen from the ground, and how Juan and Christian had hysterically relayed the tale.

He claimed it spun and spun, never stopping. The boy apparently climbed on top of it, was flung off, and hit his head on the rocky terrain. Marco looked toward the peaks of the mountains, where this aberration was located. He could not see through the trees and brush, but knew it was there taunting him.

Marco's forearms flexed as he gripped the outdoor railing. It was rusted and worn, something he would need to definitely fix. Marco was the unhandy man, with so many repairs and so little time. Sheila was—like her mother—beginning to pester him about fixing things around the house. He honestly tried his best, but just wasn't very good with manual labor.

He wished he could have been there to catch the boy, but then again, regret is the ugly stepsister of remorse. The two fell together like Jack and Jill. It was best not to reflect on the trauma and shadow the good times they'd shared, albeit short and few. Instead, he pondered the forest and its greenery, how it engulfed this machine, hid it from the world. How secretive—no, mysterious—the world can be at times. Wonders remain to be discovered and this, Marco believed, could be one of those gone unexplained.

How a machine could come from the ground, breaking through rock, amazed Marco. Though, the thought also horrified. From what source did this spire arise? What controlled it? For surely people manned machines. Scariest of all, what triggered its initiation?

Marco took the final sip of water and placed it on the side table. The forest of El Chapparal chirped with wildlife and a thrust flitted from branch to branch amongst the trees. His mind trailed back to the metal atrocity, the anomaly in the midst of the natural. Marco wondered if the animals had noticed, or were they so used to random human interference that one more machine popping out of oblivion just became another adaptation.

The thrust batted up toward heaven, dipping and rising as it saw fit. It flew higher, toward the top of the mountain, and then it became so small that it disappeared amongst the evergreen. The chirping continued unabated.

His eyes wandered over the vast green, the protected forest in one of the most beautiful and natural places left in the world, and he was glad it was directly in his backyard. Anytime he felt blue or lonely, nature was right there to warm him up. Thinking of nature automatically brought him back to Ernesto, and how death is an unavoidable part of nature. Yet, his death was so unnatural, thought Marco. He slammed his palms on the copper railing and his wedding ring sounded off the metal.

He spun the ring on his finger—going on five years—and entered the condo of waking light. He sat down on the couch and flipped on the television. On the screen a newsman was blubbering of some gruesome scene near Culver City, California. How the following footage was "not for those of a weak stomach or mind," and he claimed "any children are urged to leave the room immediately."

Marco leaned forward on the couch and squinted at the screen. There was a video recording of a traffic jam, two cars had collided. Rising from the ground was a metal spire. It spun slowly at first, but picked up speed. Then, Marco noticed a man was on top. It spun so fast that when the man jumped, his leg was torn clean off. Marco gagged as he witnessed the blood and skin fly about, over pedestrians and cars alike. Then, there was mass panic. The newsman proclaimed that several were injured and two more were killed in the frenzy.

Marco switched the channel. Three stations were out of commission. He found another broadcast from China. The spire was much taller than the one in California, maybe thirty feet high, and large arms with fan-like appendages jutted periodically from the sides of it. Marco's throat tightened, while his foot tapped on the carpet. The caption said the spire was clocked moving at one hundred and ninety miles an hour.

The newsman sent the feed over to the live anchor.

"Yeah, Chris, this thing has been crazy. It never stops. Right now, we're going to pan down to show the bomb squad moving in. We aren't sure whether these things are weapon of mass destruction or what, but in this day and age we can't be too careful."

The camera slid over to a man in an oversized astronaut's suit. He crept forward slowly, cautiously. Marco also crept forward in his seat, entranced by the scene.

The expert stopped within twenty feet of the monstrosity. He lifted his leg as if to take another step and paused. For a few moments he stood motionless as a statue. Then, the helmet started to melt like butter. The suit washed off of his body as liquid petroleum, until all that was left standing was a skeleton dipped in skin. His hair was burned into crispy black strips of seaweed. The newsman looked over his shoulder, as the camera started to shake.

He started. "For Christ's sake!" His hand knocked the camera down. The viewfinder looked at a pair of Adidas, and then faded out.

Marco's mouth hung agape. He clicked off the television and rushed to the balcony. The forest was still chirping, but now with the voices of many more winged creatures. Overlapping the subtle whine of insect legs and tired birds, an in-tune humming persisted, which burned in Marco's eardrums.

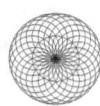

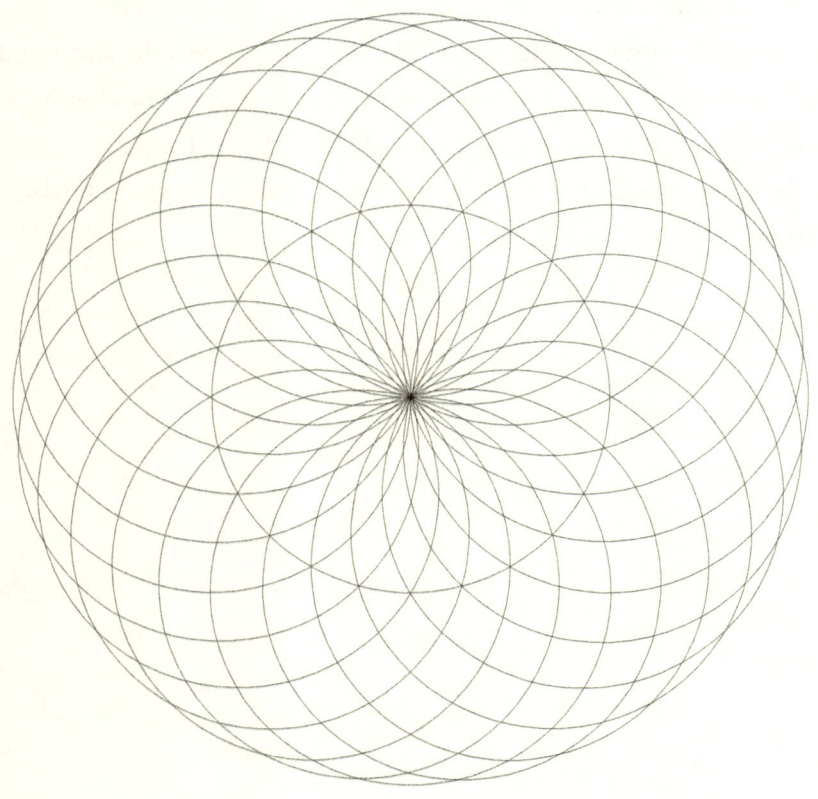

Chapter 6

EARTHEN BEINGS

Sheila was awoken by two desperately digging hands. She wondered what time it was as she sat up in bed and wiped the sand from her eyes. The room was dark and the only light was shed from the closet and the thin sheets poking out from behind the curtains. Her husband was bent over in the closet, and on the ground was an overflowing bag, which Marco tried to stuff even more clothes into.

Sheila's throat was dry as a pile of dead leaves. "Honey... what are you doing?"

Marco didn't respond at first; he just continued packing. Sheila got off the bed, which creaked opposition. The wooden floor was cold on her feet, yet they stuck to it with warm perspiration. She entered the closet and grabbed his arm. Marco whirled around with wide eyes. She noticed his chest rising and collapsing. Sweat poisoned his forehead like thin oil.

"We have to go... we have to get away from that *thing*." Marco pointed at the wall, as if he was reaching beyond the boundaries of the house, beyond the sanctity of a well-fed and nurturing home.

"What are you talking about? You're acting crazy!"

Marco pushed past Sheila, who stood in the closet door, and sat heavily on the edge of the unmade bed. "That machine... isn't the only one. There are more like it coming out of the ground everywhere. On the news I saw one in China thirty feet tall. It *melted* a man."

"Hold on, hold on," Sheila said, confused. "It *melted* him?"

Marco nodded and licked his lips. "He was a bomb expert, trying to get closer to it, but his suit melted like a candle. All that was left was a skeleton."

Sheila's stomach growled as she pictured a skeleton standing there, melted to the ground, mouth wide in an endless scream—someone's husband, son, brother. "Don't you think if there was any danger Phillip would have let us known?"

Marco slapped the mattress. "No! That guy is useless! He couldn't catch a common cold—I don't know how he was elected Sheriff. I'm telling you, we need to get away."

Sheila shushed him and rubbed his temples. Eventually, his breath slowed and he closed his eyes. The rubbing took away all the tension, she knew, just to have her hands on him. If she removed them, all the worry would resurface. It was a gift, and connection, that she knew how to soothe him.

"We just got home from being away. Why don't you just come to bed with me?" She tugged on his bare bicep. "C'mon."

He reluctantly crawled into bed with her. His muscled arms wrapped over her breasts and she felt safe. Sheila put her hand over his and held it. The back of her knees met with the front of his, and then she was out cold.

Marco could hear her breath wheezing calmly, peacefully. His eyes shifted to the window, next to the dresser. The curtains flapped lightly in the night chill, and close enough to be outside his window was the tip of the highest mountain peak.

He wished he could go to the top and stamp the evil thing into the ground. In the purple sky a form flew above the greenery, just a miniscule shadow drifting about, too steady to be a bat. The thrust flew carefully over the forest and up the side of the mountain. As it came over the peak, it dropped in mid-air.

Marco could feel his palms wet and clammy against his wife's bosom. He kissed her on the cheek and eased out of bed, careful not to wake her. His shoes were laced too tight. He threw on a sweater and closed the front door without as much as a click.

The night was sticky, despite the chilly wind which had blown into the condo. No lights were on in the village. It was strange to Marco that he felt as if he was doing something wrong. He crept through the shadows with his head low. When he reached the edge of the forest, it was pitch black. He could not see into the wooded world and it frightened him.

He had never actually been into the forest—it being a guarded preserve, one needs permission—but, growing up he'd navigated his backyard woods to the point of utter memorization. These trees were much more daunting and seemed, to Marco, to be alive. The leaves bobbed and fancied each other with their tips. The branches creaked from the long still they had endured. He recalled a specific time, after leaving his backyard as a boy, when a tick had bitten into his calf. This memory made him walk tall through the dark thicket.

Marco's feet crunched lonely in the wild and he wondered if any animals were there watching him. The thought disturbed him, the vulnerability of his situation, how some animals could see him with their night vision eyes. It made him think of a story he had read, "The Most Dangerous Game", in which the narrator is hunted for sport. Any second a wild beast—or a man, for that matter—could attack in the pitch black, and he would never sense the onslaught.

Twigs snapped beneath his shoes and leaves crunched, rocks interrupted his stealth. It was a real walk in the woods, a man alone in a terrain unknown. Marco tripped over a vine, which snagged his ankle and nearly made him fall. His elbow was punctured from a thorn on an unseen plant.

Far off an owl hooted. To Marco it was a hollow sound, as if a man had yelled "Who?" down the middle of a concrete tunnel.

He felt alone and scared, yet somehow there was a small level of comfort in the forest. He started to feel like he belonged to it. Soon, the vines would start to crawl up his legs, the trees would bear hug him, and Marco would mesh into nature.

Marco pictured his veins flowing with sap, branches growing from his abdomen, and birds nesting within his dark black hair. He would be cycled back unto the Earth from which he had been born. The skin off his bones would become the moss on the stones, and the blood of his veins would morph into Mother Nature's own sweet groundwater. As he knew it would one day happen to him, it had already happened to Ernesto. He was already in the process of being recycled. From the second he was lowered into the ground, and those flesh-eating bacteria had seeped through the pores in the wood, Ernesto had been claimed by Mother Earth. She was once more his protector.

Marco was not ready . With all the animals in the woods and the pit-falls in the dark, it could happen. He second guessed his intention in the forest of birch and oak, and could not succumb to a proper purpose. There was that machine up on the mountain, churning. What did he think he could accomplish by going to it? He knew he wouldn't be able to stop whatever the force was at work. That Chinese man...

As if the thought had been just boiling under his skin, he wanted out of the forest desperate. The way back was clouded, but he could see through the branches a hint of civilization. However, through his anxiety the trees were taking the liberty of crowding close together. Marco ran, panting, his mind dragging the trees together, forming a barrier ahead of him.

He slowed to a stop, realizing the ridiculousness of his panic. His mind expanded from its former thin ball and his vision regrouped. The exit was now three dimensional and full. Marco wondered what had possessed him to enter the woods in the first place. Not half an hour ago, he had been packing to get away from it, now he was attempting to get nearer. His navigation was all off. Going after a dangerous and unknown machine from the ground, would not bring closure to Ernesto's death. What he needed to do was put it off his brain, no matter how painful. For, seeing the machine again would resurface the problem.

Marco was moving along, until a nearby rustle caught his ear. He stopped and listened, wanted to make sure it wasn't his shoes. When the rustling continued, Marco turned slowly, not wanting to alarm what-ever—or whoever—happened to be there spying.

The woods were filled with yellow eyes of night creatures. He did not want to meet any of them. He knew that eye contact means an attempt to establish dominancy, when really he just wanted to get the hell out and go home. These eyes didn't move, but stared on at him, locked. They peered and blinked from all around, but he was so close to the forest border. If he could just back up—the bushes started to rustle again and some of the eyes vanished in a blink. Marco was off like a light.

The village engulfed him and never did he glance over his shoulder, until he was safe behind closed doors. Marco panted as he peered through the peephole. There was nothing there.

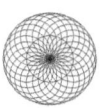

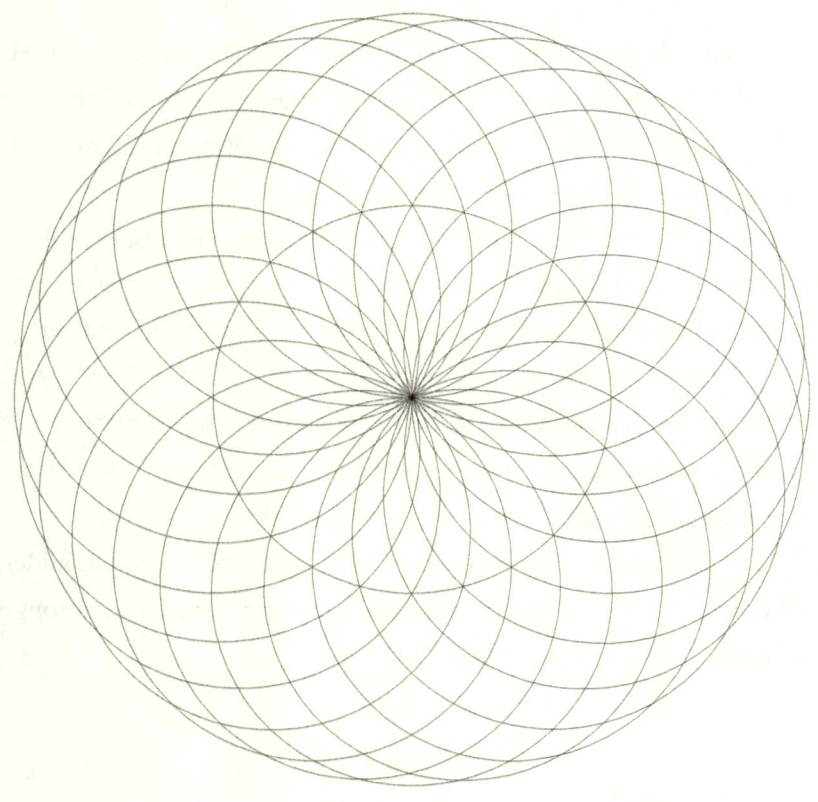

30

Chapter 7

RUNNING ON EMPTY

"Hold it down at twenty knots," Captain Portis said. He left the quarters and plodded along the promenade. Off portside, a herd of dolphins jumped and dove into the ocean, cackling and playing. The water gleamed in the sun, reflecting the far-off star that is the sun. Portis leaned both elbows on the rail, dreaming of the warmth of the Caribbean. Once they docked in the Bahamas, he could throw on a pair of swim shorts and take a dip.

Until then it was just another day aboard the S.S. Commercial. Materialism is impossible to escape, even out on the open sea. It follows you everywhere, he thought. While he sucked in the serenity above the hulk, below the deck casinos stole and shopping malls robbed, and the drink waitresses bogeyed your pockets for nine dollars a shot.

The ship was trucking through the tropic Atlantic, breezing along at a steady twenty three miles an hour. The smell of salt and suntan lotion was in the air. It reminded Portis of the beach, and why shouldn't it? He wanted to stop and stay awhile upon the island, take a short vacation, but he had a vessel to run. Besides, wasn't he always on vacation?

Portis tightened his lapels and focused his attention upon the bow, where a group of passengers had pooled. Cameras were out and flashes were disposing. He clasped his hands behind his straightened back and leisurely strolled toward the front of the ship along the navigational bridge. Tourists are always amazed by the dolphins, but to Portis the creatures were as common as squirrels in New England.

The wind whipped at his back and nearly tore the hat from his head. People were pointing toward the bow of the ship and Portis's curiosity peaked. His steps grew closer together, until he was nearly jogging. He descended the metal stairs in moments and when close enough, peered over the shoulder of a small Asian woman whose camera snapped repeatedly.

About a mile out (Portis could gauge these sorts of things from years on the leagues) something was standing out of the water. It was tall and cylindrical, and spun clockwise. Around it, the water swirled like a whirlpool, causing massive waves.

Portis recoiled. He tore ass down the promenade, whilst over his walkie-talkie ordering "Shut the thrusters off!" The wooden deck took the abuse of his shoes. He hadn't run that much since high school track, and it was apparent by his lack of breath. The door opened for him just as he came to the top of the metal stairwell.

It was Peter who was holding the door for his entrance. "Pete!" He panted. "There's something ahead of us—creating a whirlpool."

Peter was the Quartermaster. He was quick to turn and adjust his orientation toward the ship automation system. He clicked on his walkie-talkie and reported to the helmsman. "Sharp left, Glenn." He stated plainly.

Pete was almost more experienced a sailor than Portis. He had navigated the Indian Ocean, Bering Sea, and Persian Gulf. The man knew his way around a boat. Out of every officer aboard, Portis trusted Peter Blair with his life. Pete looked over the automation system's screen. "That wasn't there a moment ago."

Portis wiped his forehead. He grabbed his walkie, pressed the "TALK" button. "Engine Control. Those turbines off?" To Portis it sounded, and felt, as if they were still burning strong. Through the front window he could see the ocean's monstrosity growing larger. It was rising from the water.

"Archambault?" When the superintendent didn't respond, Portis turned on the CCTV above his head.

"Holy shit." Pete covered his mouth with his hand.

Portis stepped away from the screen and plopped into the leather chair at the controls. The men were dead on the floor, some were draped over their computers. On the passenger decks, everyone was dead. The casino ran on empty. A dealer was laid across a roulette table, leaking blood from the ears, his irises the color of fine wine.

The captain flipped through each channel. Every floor below the promenade was void of life, or rather, robbed of it. "What the fuck is happening?" Pete asked his leader.

Portis grasped his chin in his hand. "Don't know, Pete, but we need to lock those damn doors."

The two could hear, coming from below deck, the powering down of the turbines and shutting off of the engine. On the cameras, the ceiling lights blinked off. Portis felt a sinking in his stomach, worse than motion sickness. A man walked down the stairs to the lower floor and as if shot by an arrow, fell dead. The automation system's screen scrambled.

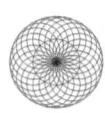

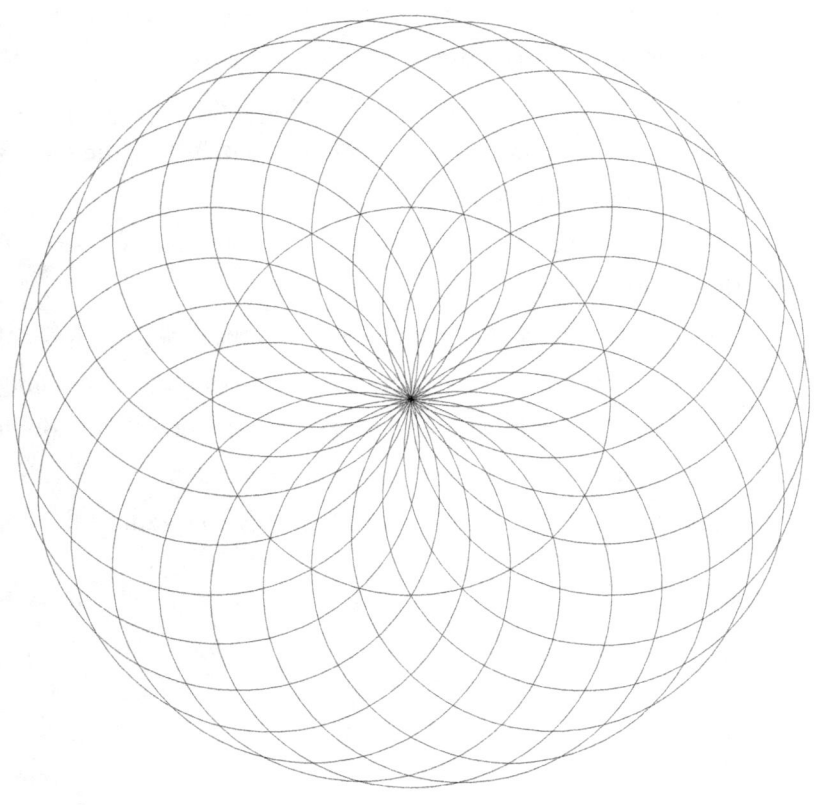

Chapter 8

SMALL EXPRESSIONS

M arco opened his eyes in a shiver. The blankets were gone from his body and goose bumps were raised over his bare chest and arms. Sheila was gone for work and the only remnant of her presence was a single strand of dirty blonde hair lying across her crumpled pillow.

He hadn't slept well, tossing and turning throughout the night, too hot for comfort. None of his usual nightmares had plagued him, but his eyelids continued to resist their much needed closure. Marco flipped onto his back and folded the pillow in half beneath his head, still uncomfortable.

Returning to the daily grind sounded awful. The satisfaction of vacation always seemed to wear off so much faster, as the realism of its absence grew clearer. The trip had been great. He and Sheila had gotten along fantastically, and he felt closer to her than he had in a long while. He missed her already and found himself snuggling into the comforter for a trace of lingering scent. Marco picked up the lavender of her shampoo, and relished in it. He curled his hand into the cotton blanket and pushed the clump under his nose. He wanted her there, just to hold, maybe to fall back asleep—if not forever, at least for just a while longer. However, the electronic alarm clock told him that it was nine forty-seven, and he had to be to work for eleven o'clock.

The hour was at call to eat and fashion some grub for himself. He reluctantly threw his legs over the side of the bed and sprang forth. He chewed down a bowl of cereal, as if it were of no consequence, and then proceeded into the shower. The first hot, fresh shower at home felt so good, and Marco found himself not wanting to exit the downpour. The water rinsed away all of the remnants of the vacation—the sand, the seaweed, the fun, all of it down the drain. It was surreal how it all disappeared like that, as if it never truly had happened at all.

He wiped his face with the towel and dried his genitals off with the bottom at the same time. Then, he threw on some khakis, a button up, and finally his apron. Marco looked at himself in the mirror. With the extra color, he didn't even recognize his own reflection. He stared deep into his twin's eyes; they looked changed as well. It's always said that people don't change, but Marco always felt that every little experience—be it near death or inconsequential—changes a person, if only slightly.

Marco got to the café at seven minutes after eleven o'clock. He had walked to work, the place being only half a mile down the dirt road. The usuals sat abreast the window (Mr. Rivera and his farmhand Nino), there every morning a ten o'clock sharp. Suarez Rivera owned the four acre goat farm at the far end of the village, selling produce and dairy to all the local businesses for cheap. Marco shot them a casual wave, accompanied with a smile.

Nino shouted "Marco!" excitedly, with a wave.

Manuel was behind the counter, leaning on the wall and picking at his nails. Marco went straight for the coffee maker and poured a tall cup of beans. Manuel's business wasn't a thriving one, but he made enough to get by. His sister owned the building and lived upstairs from the café. So, running the business didn't extract from his pocket too much. Marco sipped the hot beverage. Manuel brewed the best cup hands down, never too strong and never watered down.

Even though Manuel was thirty years Marco's senior, he had become Marco's best friend. "How was your trip?" Manuel asked.

One of the reasons they had become so close, Marco assumed, was Manuel's clear English. It made for an easy transition to the country. Marco stretched his spine, still stiff from the long hours in the car.

"It was good. We got to visit my uncle, Ricardo, which was great because I hadn't seen him for years. Then, we spent a lot of time on the beach after that, of Sheila's choosing."

Manuel nodded with satisfaction. "Get used to it my friend."

He smiled because he knew more than Marco. His wife Petra had passed two years beforehand and not a day went by that Manuel didn't bring her up. The events with Ernesto had carried it all to the surface, Marco could tell by Manuel's subdued behavior. She had been a good woman to him. Manuel had many beautiful stories. Thinking of this made him smile.

Petra had been his best friend and companion for thirty years. They had seen the world together. Some people from Montejo never leave the farming town, even on vacation. Manuel and Petra had made a point to get out, break the mold. He claimed she was one of the good ones. He talked of her as one of the only wise people in the world, always touting that humans are inherently stupid. She was the exact opposite, she was born of wisdom, he would say.

"Women rule this world, regardless of title. It is not the great men who make decisions, but the women behind them, wagging their fingers." Manuel wagged his own finger at Marco with a smile. He could always be counted on to bring a smile to your face or a small tidbit to philosophize.

"How was the cafe without me?" Marco asked.

"Oh, you know I don't need you." Manuel ribbed Marco with his elbow. "Really... nothing special happened. I've been getting along just fine." The older man sipped his coffee. Then, he started to wipe the dishes with a rag. Marco could hear him wheezing from just the weak effort.

He headed into the back room where every morning either Manuel, or himself, rolled the pastries. Marco cracked his knuckles and opened the sliding refrigerator cabinet. There was a large tray filled with sugared dough for the Danishes. He extracted the fresh fruit. Before he could start to knead the dough, however, the front door's bell jangled.

Marco peeked from the small pantry to see who had entered. It was Sheriff Phillip. His pockets held his fingers hostage, as he approached the counter. Marco was curious to know what it was all about, for rarely did Phillip come into the cafe, and with the recent developments he was sure no good had arisen. Marco dusted his hands on his apron and walked behind the counter.

Sheriff Phillip was talking lightly to Manuel, whose face provided no comic relief. He simply nodded, listening intently. Marco slowly poured a fresh cup of coffee, while eavesdropping. He spoke in Spanish, but Marco interpreted in his head.

"... they will be riding up today. Ranger Ana and I are going to escort them. I'll tell you, Manuel. This thing has got us all freaked out. Nobody has any idea of what they are or where they came from."

Marco tuned the rest out. When the police are freaked out, there is a cause for concern. They are supposed to keep the order and justice. It's what they're hired to do, he thought. If they aren't able to, then who is? Plus, after what he'd seen from the channel in China, Marco wasn't sure the rangers—or whoever these secret helpers were—could do anything about these oddities. He just couldn't shake that image of a melting man. It made him wonder just what other capabilities these machines had.

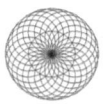

Chapter 9

UP ON THE MOUNTAIN

Sheriff Phillip Belize led the group that consisted of six men and one woman (Ranger Ana Silva) through the horse trails and up the side of the mountain. At most points the trails were dangerously steep and it was far easier to utilize the animals, rather than traveling by foot.

Rooney, Phillip's horse, stepped around a large boulder quickly and nearly lost its balance. The trail following the boulder became almost a straight vertical plane. Phillip had traveled the treacherous path many times, but it was never a simple task.

He pulled on the reigns, so that Rooney would slow down. No need to rush. A fall down the hill would likely be a death trap. He figured the boys must have gone through the forest itself. They must have been playing on the mountain and stumbled upon the obscurity.

The sun was beating down fierce, turning grasses and bushes brown in the summer. It ripened the holly past its light red, until the balls looked more like cranberries. Ranger Belize imagined the holly berries bursting from the excess of juice, the liquid running down the side of the mountain like blood.

Ana followed the pack, making sure none of the agents slowed, or accidentally veered off the path. Directly in front of her was Agent Solzhein, who she found rather handsome. They had been talking on the way up the mountain. Ana came to the conclusion that he was attractive not only in body, but also in spirit.

"How long have you been working for Spain?" she asked in her thick accent.

"About three years. I came to this country because it was a beautiful place. I never wanted to leave." His accent was equally as thick, but came with a Germanic tone.

Ana watched him as he trailed alongside. His stern expression was somehow gentle, absent of anger. She thought maybe he was making the face, not out of angst, but from the relentless heat. The humidity was low, but the dry heat could be just as bad if you weren't hydrated.

"I've lived here most of my life. It is a beautiful country, especially here in these mountains. They are the reason I became a park ranger."

Solzhein swung around to look at her. He bobbed up and down from the horse's motions. "You have lived in this city for your entire life?"

"Oh, no. I grew up in a town next to Barcelona, a very similar village, probably why I grew so fond of it."

The group reached the crest of the hill and stopped. Rooney was causing a commotion. It whinnied, bucked, and then reared onto its hind legs.

"Woah, nino! Relajar!" Belize said. He rubbed Rooney's ears as he did so often to calm the beast, but it wouldn't cooperate. Rooney stood tall and flung Phillip to the rocky surface. The Sheriff landed on top of his wrist, which curled with a crunch.

Phillip rolled over onto his back. Ana jumped off her horse's back and rushed to his assistance. As Rooney galloped past, Ana's horse, Princess, joined him and they tore ass down the mountain. Ana crouched down next to Phillip, who was cursing his limp left hand. She grabbed her friend around the shoulder and assisted him to his feet.

"Joder! It hurts, Ana." He tried to prop the limp arm up with his other hand and screamed.

"Solzhein?" Ana asked.

"Yes?" He trotted over on his horse, which was also beginning to buck.

"Can you bring Phillip back to our camp, por favor?"

"Of course."

Solzhein grabbed Phillip by the good hand and pulled him onto the saddle, while Ana shoved his large rear. Her superior let tears shamelessly leak from their ducts. He gave Ana a small wave to say "Don't worry about me," and the pair rode off down the mountain.

After ten minutes of travel the road began to curve slightly left and uphill. Ana was walking on foot, but in order to make it safely down the mountain, she would need to ride one of the Legionnaire's horses. They had agreed to guide the agents in the correct direction, but never alleged to go near the oddity. Besides, they were Montejo's animals. She could steal them away at any time.

The ground vibrated as they grew closer, rumbling with the rotation of the machine. On a typical day the air was thinner at the top of the mountain, however, on the particular day oxygen seemed absent altogether. It was difficult to breathe, every step was winding Ana. She decided to go no farther, and that the time was at hand to check on her friend, Phillip.

"It's right up this hill." Ana switched on her charm and gave the agent (she couldn't remember his name, but thought it was Jim) puppy dog eyes. Then again, didn't they always use generic and fabricated names, these governmental workers?

"Do you think I could borrow your horse? You could ride with him?" She indicated another of the agents with her thumb.

Jim seemed skeptical, but he caved after a few more minutes of her intense gaze, softening to her beauty and breaking. "Sure thing, sweetheart." He swung one long leg off the horse.

She noticed he stood almost two heads taller.

"Thank you so much." Giving him a wink, she climbed onto the saddle. She knew they were most likely checking out her ass in the tight green ranger shorts, as she mounted the beast.

As Cinnamon trotted away from the isolated agents, she found herself worrying for everyone. She worried for Phillip and his broken wrist, the agents dealing with the machine, Princess and Rooney, and for herself— having to navigate the trails alone in the waning hours of daylight. Ana had always felt at home in the forest, but after feeling the vibrations and hearing the continual humming the spin created, she felt anything but comfortable within the bounds of nature's prison.

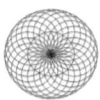

Marco had known it was a terrible idea for them to go up the mountain. Not only had Phillip broken his wrist, but none of the five other agents had returned from their investigation. A search party had gathered. Marco reluctantly volunteered. Sheila had opted to stay at home, never much for hiking. Manuel would have gone—it was certainly in his heart to do so—but, with his heart and increasingly bad asthma, it would be against his better judgment.

They met at the church, where Ranger Ana, Father Cruz, Mr. Rivera's wife, and Nino stood. Ana held a machete and a flashlight. Father Cruz was dressed down in jeans and a long sleeved shirt.

"*Marco, you should probably put some pants on,*" Father Cruz said, as Marco waded toward the group.

Marco had considered it, but decided since the heat was peaked at an unusual one hundred and three degrees that shorts would prevent overheating, sweating, and itching.

"*It's too hot, Father. This is fainting weather,*" Marco responded in Spanish.

Father Cruz's eyes smiled behind his glasses. His were the type you could look into and lose all fear. Even if you weren't a believer, or were of a non-religious denomination, Marco believed Father Cruz could turn your heart.

"Pack one hundred people into my church. Now that's fainting weather. It's all about hydration."

Of course, he was right. Marco had readied a backpack full of waters, threw in a compass, and a flashlight for good measure. Since there was no indication of when they would return, a compass could prove a vital tool. There were stories of El Chapparal, of strange noises and creatures unknown to man. People had gone missing inside the thicket, and he certainly didn't want to become one of the lost. It would be just his luck to never return home.

Ranger Ana addressed the small rescue team. *"Last I knew... they were at the top of the mountain. We have no idea of what these things are capable. They could be bombs, and that's why we should treat them as such."*

"If they were bombs, shouldn't we call bomb specialists? Some sort of professionals?" asked Nino.

"We are not going to investigate the machine. We're simply looking for the Legionnaire agents... they were the professionals."

Ana bent down and pulled her shoe laces tight, crossed them for comfort. Marco looked away, for her shirt hung too low and he could see her bra. He felt blasphemous standing next to Father Cruz and witnessing it. She stood up straight and Marco returned his attention.

"We should split up, no?" she asked in native tongue.

Nino said, *"I'll go with Marco."*

Father Cruz decided to accompany Mrs. Rivera and Ana, so two women would not need to bear the elements alone, always a gentleman. The split left Marco and Nino without machete, even more so Marco wished he had worn pants.

After the split, Nino walked beside Marco, through dirt reflecting sand crystals. The bell in the church tower let them know it was two in the afternoon. It would have been Father Devante pulling the rope and signaling the traditional town of the time.

Marco looked at Nino's skin—almost as brown as an African's—and found himself wishing he'd applied sunscreen. Despite his tolerance to the rays, long exposure still burnt his pigmented form. The mid-afternoon sun would certainly dry him up if he didn't hydrate.

"*Do you think we'll find them?*" Nino asked, after they'd broken far enough off.

Marco assumed the men were lost. Deep in his stomach he could feel that something terrible had happened to them, and despite this, he wanted to pursue them. He felt universally tied to the machine. Marco constantly needed stimulation, and had he skipped out on the expedition, would have felt like something important had been missed.

"*No. I think they're dead. I can feel it on the air… can't you? The whole mountainside feels shrouded in it.*"

"*Yeah, I guess I can. What did you come for, then?*"

It was a worthy question and Marco assumed he could answer for both of them. When something beyond the realm of comprehension occurs, everyone wants in, either for personal reassurance or monetary gain. The world being such a nosy place, everyone needs to know everything, even if it doesn't concern them.

Nino pushed forward up the steep incline, his thick anchors of legs weighing him to the surface of the Earth, not allowing him to float away. "*I came to see it,*" he stated casually, as if it were just a giraffe at the zoo.

"*Things like this don't happen here. It's like murder. Here, in our town, it changes the way everyone sees things—especially other people.*"

Marco took it in. In California, murders were so commonplace that one couldn't turn on the news without word of death. Yet, nothing to this magnitude happened. Sure there were "UFO" sightings (being relatively close to Area 51) and natural disasters, but this was like a mix of the two, minus the little green space men.

Nino continued in his native tongue. *"I know a lot about this kind of stuff. I'm always reading up on it. Personally, I need to see this firsthand. Someday I'm going to be an Archaeologist. So, how could I let an opportunity like this slide right away?"*

Marco's reasoning was much closer to his heart. Any type of knowledge he could gain regarding the machine was good, but he wanted to gauge the danger of this machine—to keep him and his wife safe. It had been one of his intentions that late night in the woods, but he was too frightened to see for himself. A search party was a great front, a perfect presentation of false comfort.

"Aren't you scared, Nino? I mean digging old shit up? What if you found something that you wish you hadn't?"

The thought visibly stung Nino. Marco's purpose wasn't to make Nino question his dreams. However, Marco couldn't help, but wonder—what lies beneath the crust of the Earth, undisturbed and in wait? He could imagine the horrors.

"I would be lying if I said no."

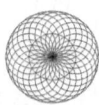

Solzhein had tracked Princess down, but couldn't find a trace of Rooney. He apologized to Sheriff Phillip, who wept not because of his broken wrist, but for the loss of a companion, pet, and friend. Solzhein offered to continue the search, but Phillip told him to carry on—the search for his companions was far more important, than that for a horse.

Thus, he saddled and reined Princess, and cantered up the mountain. She obeyed him well enough, despite the anxiousness she had displayed the previous day. Princess was a strong creature, Solzhein thought, and could have passed for a work horse any other time and place.

"Good girl," he told her, while bobbing on her back. He looked pensively about the dreamland forest. The way the hills rolled gently, falling close enough unto each other to remind one of a pan full of pastries. Even the grass seemed to sway hypnotically, endearing your eyes toward the ground.

The wind had abated and the air was significantly less humid than the past few days, but the dry heat was alternately wicked. It made breathing a fruitless task, where with humidity it felt like you were inhaling rainwater. Solzhein was accustomed to the dreary days of wet England. He had been living in the United Kingdom before moving to Spain—and was still adapting to the extreme weather—but grew up in Bavaria. A very convoluted history, he knew, but these were the things he wanted to tell Ana. He wanted to pour his heart out to her over a romantic dinner, lead her into the bedroom, and make passionate love to her.

Solzhein longed to stare into her green eyes. Subconsciously, his heels dug deeper into the sides of Princess and the horse picked up speed. He leaned forward in the saddle when the horse steadied to a brisk trot. Ahead a stream presented a trite obstacle, which Princess jumped with ample grace. They landed on the other side without interruption. Solzhein allowed the horse to travel in this fashion for a good half an hour, needing to bridge the distance they were behind the search party. He knew it couldn't be much farther. He surveyed the canopy of trees on the mountainside for any sign of movement.

On the incline before him there was a flickering of branches, too exaggerated for the wind. He followed the lead, pushing Princess to her limit. Solzhein ducked behind her neck for fear of being thrown from her back by a low hung arm of a tree. The woods were darkened when he left the path, trees sewn together by the tight thread of unabashed nature. A form was moving quickly through the brush, another horse. Like himself, the rider was slumped forward in the saddle. He couldn't tell who it was, but could tell by the uniform that it was one of the Legion.

He dug his heels in and Princess kicked up dirt. They were directly behind the rider and Solzhein steered Princess to the left. The horse ahead, drove as if the Headless Horseman was its passenger. Solzhein wondered why the other man wouldn't stop or slow.

He yelled "Hey!" over the sound of trampling hooves, but to no avail. Was the agent passed out, injured, dead? Solzhein nearly jammed his heel through the animal's stomach. Princess whined with the pressure. Once beside the other horse, Solzhein grabbed the reins and was able to slow the animal to cessation. It offered him no comfort. When the horse was completely stopped, Jim's head rolled to the side, presenting Solzhein with a skeletal face.

His skin, eyes, and bones were all intact. However, his skin was tightly stretched over his face, light blue and leathery. Jim's arm swung limply over the horse's side like a pendulum. His body was thinner, and his eyes were sunken into his gaunt face. He could barely be called a body. It was as if the life force had been sucked clean out.

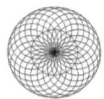

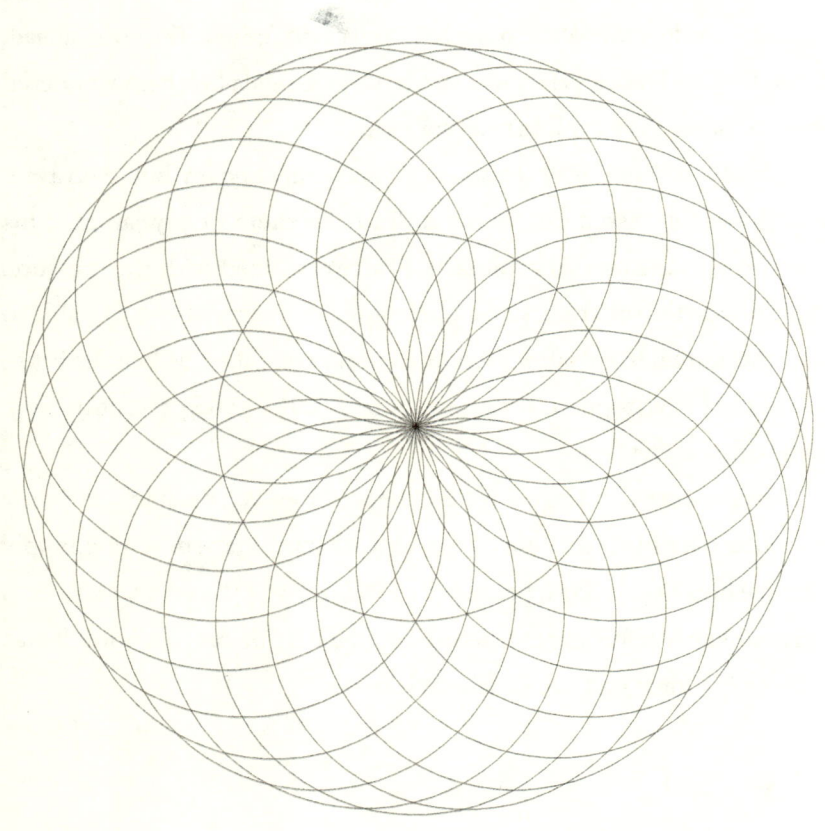

Chapter 10

WEATHER THE STORM

"They're all locked," Pete said.

"Good. So nobody can get down there, then?"

"Not a soul."

Portis stood and looked at the growing crowd. The phone started to ring. Portis picked up the receiver. It was Mary, the purser, responsible for the welfare of passengers. "Captain?" she asked.

"Yes?"

"It's me, Mary."

"I can see. I know what you're going to tell me, but I have no idea what to do. In order to turn, we would need to switch the engines on."

There was a worried sigh on the other end of the line. Portis said "We can't get send out any distress signals either."

It was widely known that Portis was viewed as a dick. Very few enjoyed his company besides Pete, but Mary was another. If anything, she had a bit of a crush on him, thus tolerating his corrosiveness. He knew of this prejudice, and oddly, it made him feel like the boss. The line between authority and friend needs to be thickly drawn.

"What should I tell them then?"

Portis couldn't be sure. He knew it wasn't quite time to deploy the lifeboats, but the time was pressing. "Tell them everything is fine, it'll pass."

The silence hung. Mary stuttered. "I.. I.. Is it true?"

Portis pursed his lips and loosened his grip on the phone. He needed to be accountable for the passengers, whether it was Mary's job or not. He was the captain. Captain covered his eyes with his hand. "I'm not sure. Forget what I said. Don't tell them anything—just say it's under control. We're working on it."

"Okay. Keep me updated, though."

"Will do, Mary."

"And Captain?"

"Yeah?"

"Please be careful."

The line clicked and Portis hung the receiver onto the cradle, covered in his sweat. Pete was in one of the navigational chairs, with his back to the Captain. His feet were crossed on top of the useless control panel and his arms wove over his chest. Portis stole the seat next to him.

"What do we do, Captain?" he asked quietly.

Pete untangled his arms and grabbed the arm of his chair. His brow was creased, and he watched the spire intently. The sky was getting darker, disposing of the early hour, speaking of grey. It looked like a brewing storm—hopefully, not a hurricane. There hadn't been a prediction of one, but in the Caribbean Portis knew they sometimes popped up virtually out of nowhere, leaving destruction in their wakes.

Pete drummed his fingers on the arms of the chair. He turned his red bearded face toward Portis. "Cap?"

Portis came free of the ocean—of his life. The wide ocean had been everything he'd known for the past ten years. All of his friends were on the ship. He tried to think of any friends he had on land, but couldn't count one. The life was all he knew.

"We do as always, Pete. We persevere."

Pete drummed some more. He was a man of action. Portis could feel the idleness wearing his old friend down.

"Should we call the Guard?"

Portis felt bad for holding back on Pete. Pete was the one man he felt comfortable talking with, confiding in. He was the one constant in his dynamic life, and keeping secrets wasn't something they did.

"We can't"

Pete sat forward, making the seat squeak, and picked up the radio. His face went slack. It was an expression Portis had never seen on the man's face in all his life—complete fear.

"I tried earlier," Portis admitted.

The captain tucked his hands in the pockets of his slacks. The phone clicked onto its cradle once more. Far off, the metal thing spun, creating giant waves. The ship started to dip and rise—not something typical of a cruise ship—and the fear hit the captain.

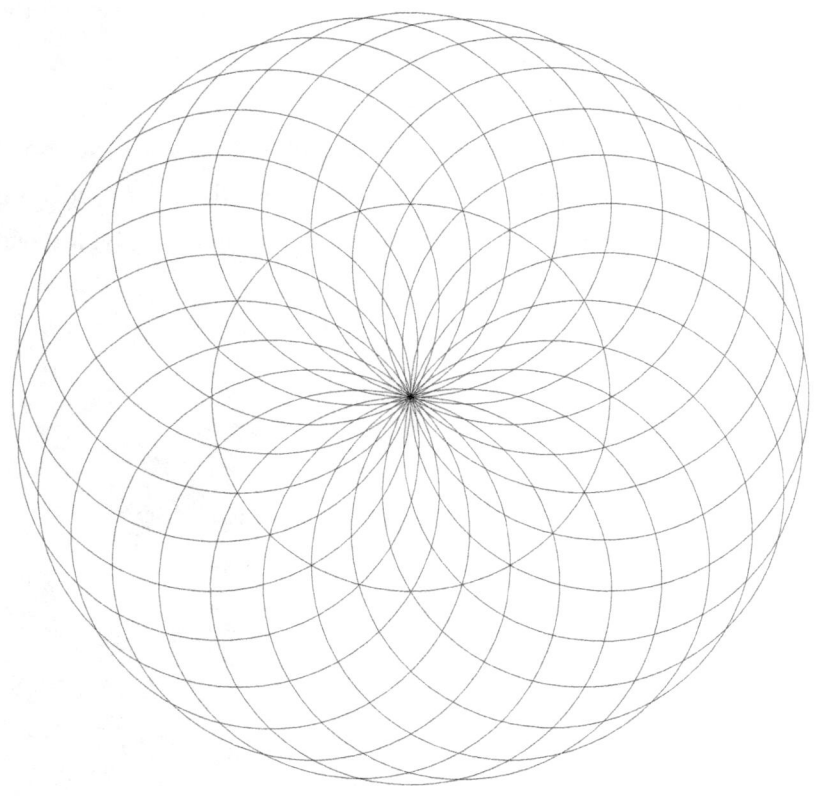

Chapter 11

THE SEARCH AND DISCOVERY

Marco trudged ahead of Nino, breaking branches and stomping ivy. Nino complained of a sore back and his fear of ticks. So, Marco was forced to head the team. What amazed him was how Nino could power the fields day in and day out for Mr. Rivera, but a walk through the woods drained all of his energy. He sized Nino up. His head was down and his feet dragged through the unstable terrain. The kid was a good ten years younger, and Marco had way more stamina.

He blamed it on technology and the world's increasing dependence. Nowadays, he thought, kids stay inside all day playing on the computer, watching television, and playing video games. Growing up, Marco had spent all of his time outdoors. The American way had slowly crept into Europe and other continents, infecting the social and personal lifestyles of traditional people. Worst of all, the parents feed into it. They use the television or computer as a babysitter while they do their own personal web surfing. It sickened Marco, and he vowed to steer his children clear of it. They will think an X-Box is a lasting piece of a plane crash.

They'd been at it over an hour, and though Marco still had strength to carry on, it seemed pointless. These were three grown, trained Legionnaires on horseback. If in danger, what could Marco do for them? They were specialized to deal with extreme circumstances, not him. From the beginning it had been a ridiculous idea, which had stemmed from curiosity.

Marco's stomach rumbled. He pulled his cell phone out and thought, hypocrite. The LCD home screen told him it was quarter after three. It also read: "NO SERVICE." His cell phone was the one piece of plastic he *was* reliant upon, and he hated the fact that it was out of commission. It had become a part of him and not being able to use it was a bit like a small anxiety attack, making him feel like he'd lost something very important, when in the scheme of things it was nothing of value. The only worth it held was the ability to contact Sheila in case of emergency, which he could not do.

"I'm almost ready to head back," Marco said. He paused and turned around.

The sweat was gathering under Nino's arms—two crescent pools blended into the cotton of his shirt. *"Tell me about it!"* He said in Spanish.

"I'm so hungry. I could go for a cheeseburger."

Nino closed his eyes and smacked his lips, dreaming of the invisible beef patty.

"Want to get one after?"

Nino opened his eyes. *"I want to get one now."*

Marco agreed and the pair turned toward town. At least the path back would be trampled, he thought, but they should have left some Reese's Pieces or something. They had strayed from the main path—which leads to the summit—and created their own route under the impression that the Legionnaires had done the same.

It wasn't more than ten minutes, by Marco's cell, before they emerged onto the main rocky road. The sound of horse hooves drummed the ground. Whoever it was had come from town. The sound grew closer, until Marco and Nino could see the dirt clouds above the trees, urgency was in the strides. Solzhein approached, curving around the path on Princess, bent down and riding hard. He wore a mask of determination and dirt. When he was within speaking distance, he yanked on the horse's reins to slow the beast.

"We *must* go back into town," he said. The urgency crept into his accented voice.

"Okay… we were headed that way, anyhow. What's happened?" Marco asked with just a tad bit of worry edging on the end of his words.

"Everything's fine in town, but I found Jim."

"And?" Nino asked.

Solzhein shook his head solemnly, but without emotion. He spoke with disgust. "I can't really explain. He was... dead, but not like any dead man I've seen before. Believe me I've seen a lot. He didn't look human. He looked fake and *empty*."

Marco had known. Two deaths in a single week, and if his premonition held true, there would be two more as of yet to be announced. It further confirmed the fact that if he and Sheila were to be safe, they needed to get the hell out of town.

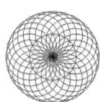

"**P**ack up," Marco said when he walked through the door.

Sheila was sitting on the couch eating popcorn, but sat up with a gasp with his powerful entrance. She was in her pajamas, and brushed the spilt corn off her lap.

"Where are we going?"

"Those agents were killed. Solzhein found one of them. He thinks the machine is emitting some sort of nuclear rays. From what I saw on the news in China, I believe him."

"So what, Marco? We get home from vacation and we're supposed to just up and leave again?"

"That would be the general idea." Marco advanced for the bedroom, started to pack the necessities. His idea was to fly to Sacramento, to make sure everything was alright with his mother. He took a break to pick up the phone. He dialed her number. From the other end a loud buzzing came, making him pull the receiver away from his ear.

He hung up the earpiece and snatched his laptop off the bureau. It took a few minutes to boot to the desktop, but once it was prepared he clicked the Internet Explorer icon. The server said: "Page Temporarily Unavailable." Then, another balloon popped up saying "Diagnose Internet Connection." Marco slowly closed the computer and placed it on the bed next to him. He could feel Sheila standing in the doorway. Her arms hung limp at her sides and one of her hips poked out farther than it should.

When he tried the television, he was unsurprised to see snow filling the thirty two inch screen. Marco's temple throbbed at a single vein. His head felt clouded. Sheila came and sat beside him, making the mattress sink lower and took his hand in hers.

"Can you relax now, sweetie? You're all worked up."

Marco's shoulder slumped, but he could feel his neck all taut with anxiety. He knew this wasn't good. All connection with the outside world was gone. It wasn't just a power outage or a lapse in coverage. It was an outage in whole, a break from society.

"I know. I can feel it in my muscles. I had a dream last night... my mother was cradling my father, dead in his arms, and she was crying blood." Marco covered his face with his hand as if to block the image. "They were sitting on top of the machine, spinning. I tried to climb it, to help them."

"So, what, do you want to go to America?"

"Yes, I really do."

Sheila let his hand go. It fell into his lap, where he spun his wedding ring around his finger.

"Why do we have to be so hasty? Can't we just wait to see if it passes? Spain is just as equipped for this sort of thing as America."

"I wish it was an easy answer. I just... I want to be *near* my mother, just in case."

"In case of what, Marco? Monsters come crawling out of it?" Sheila wore a mocking smile.

Marco wished he could wipe it off of her face. "You're always so disbelieving. If you had seen what I had, you wouldn't be acting like this."

"If you're so scared, then why did you join the search party?"

The question was a good one and struck Marco in many different places. It could have been his compassion for the others, or his want for closure, but it was still not a solid answer. For Marco it was oddly complicated.

"Somehow I feel drawn to it."

Sheila widened her eyes. "O… kay, ya' creep."

"No, you don't get it. I feel somewhat responsible—like if I had been here, everything would have been just fine. I could have stopped the boys from going up there. We may have never known about it and we could have gone on living uninterrupted."

Sheila gave a short, uninspired laugh. "I swear, sometimes you have this messiah complex. *I'm here, everything is fine!*"

Marco guessed it was a little grandiose. What could he really have done to stop them? Young boys are going to do what they want. If not when he was around, then when he was at work. Besides, he's not their father. Marco knew rebellion to be an instinct of the growing boy. He was bred with it plentifully as any other, and learned to use it to his advantage. Marco came to find that women love the sensitive rebel, Sheila being no exception. She loved when he acted tough, especially for her honor.

"I'm not trying to say that everyone looks to me for guidance, like I'm some sort of leader, just that I feel like I could have helped prevent it."

As if Sheila remembered then what it was he wanted to prevent, the silence dulled her smile, until it all but faded. It turned into a fake representation and she even catered to the nullification of that.

"I want to go check on my mother, Sheila. I want to see if there is a better situation over there, as well… for us. If you're not coming I'm going anyway."

Her head whipped around. "You would really go without me?"

He thought about if he had truly meant it. Would he leave her at such a time? His own mind wanted to slap him across the face. There was no way he could ever, and was disgusted to have even considered. A quick answer should have been in order.

"No… I would never."

Marco wrapped his arm over her shoulders and she kissed the back of his hairy hand. He rubbed her ear lobe and moved to her neck. She nuzzled back with the side of her face.

"I was just testing you."

They sat like that for a good five minutes, until Sheila stood and walked to the closet. She grabbed several dresses, a few blouses—always have to look good. Marco laid back and tried to relax for a moment. Sheila continued to pack and get ready. Her movements became little more than mice in the wall as Marco started to drift, but all he could really hear and feel, was the steady hum of that damn machine.

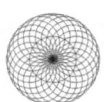

Chapter 12

AMERICA THE GRANDIOSE

A brown eye peeked through the blinds, next to a fat finger with a long nail, and then the blind clicked shut. The streets were vacant of life, countless Americans holed up in their houses, fearful of what lay outside. There was the occasional National Guard truck driving by, albeit rarely.

It was unusually hot in Laguna, the air full of humidity rather than the typical dry heat exhibited in Southern California—the desert heat. Sal had the air conditioning on full blast while he sat in his condo awaiting further orders. He was glad it still worked, for the temperatures were climbing toward one-ten.

The last time the television had been operable the President had declared a National State of Emergency and requested the citizens of America to remain indoors. He claimed no areas of the country were exempt from this piece of advice, unless to shop for provisions. A spire had popped up in virtually every populous region—thousands, millions of them.

Sal spent his time writing in his journal and playing cards and video games, but it was getting boring being cooped up all day. The firm had stayed open, but Sal refused to go to work. He wasn't sure what the repercussions of contact with the machines were, and until they were discovered, there was no chance of him working at the firm.

Footage had been leaked of humans who were living too close to the machines (the newscaster had said less than half a mile), and they were deformed to a point of no recognition. It was nothing like Sal had ever seen before. AIDs patients looked drained, but these people looked fabricated, like something from a B-horror movie with awful special effects. They looked like live wax figures, their faces barely holding onto the bone, eyes yellowed to almost brown. One woman was pulling her hair out in bloody clumps, her nails breaking loose as she dug across her scalp.

Sal constantly checked his own body for signs of ailment, running his fingers through his short hair, inspecting every inch of his body for bruises, chafing. He was a little over a mile to the nearest machine, but Sal was a hypochondriac. He thought coffee would give him a heart attack.

The worry was giving him cabin fever, and he even worried the worry would lead to agoraphobia. He clicked the blinds open again—still, nobody was out there. It had been almost a week since their surfacing, and since then Sal had only seen twenty-two cars drive by. Sal thought that maybe they were fearful of driving *into* one of the atrocities, by how cautious and slow they traveled.

His cabinets were full of canned goods, but he was running low on milk and bread. Would the grocery store even have any, he wondered? Then, he dismissed the thought. *Of course, they would. Just because people are scared to go outside, it's not the end of the world.*

Sal's house sat on the corner of two main roads and where they intersected, his house sat up on its hill. The neighborhood was deathly quiet compared to normal and as Sal worked his way down the driveway, he noticed a small tricycle tipped on its side. The wheel spun in mid-air from the passing breath of God. He wondered where the little boy or girl was, the owner, if they were even alive. If they were, would they have the energy to ride such a piece of equipment?

He hopped into his Porsche and powered up. It worked just fine despite the prolonged stagnancy, and he revved the engine a couple of times. He checked the mirrors, making sure they were in place and his visibility was good, and flicked on the GPS. The screen scrambled like an egg, the voice like a far-off alien transmission.

"Kssh… wel… goeemm… ksssh…"

Sal flipped the thing off, better not to think about it. The car started to move, while he was determining which direction to go. The nearest machine was also near the most convenient grocery store, half a mile away. He decided the best choice was to take the long trip across town—where people may be alive and moving. Where maybe there was not one of the strange harbingers.

Sal pushed his foot onto the accelerator, felt the tug of the engine as the car pulsed ahead. No cars passed on either side, and Sal felt the car casually drifting into the left lane. He hadn't been sleeping well and the lack thereof forced him to steer hard to the right. The machines were ever present, distracting his brain, holding his eyelids open like windows in the Spring. He buzzed the window down into the doorframe and perched his arm on the sill. The air would keep him awake.

A young woman stood in the yard of a small blue ranch. Her attention swung with the passing vehicle, even as her watering can drowned her dying lilacs, burnt and withering in the unrelenting sun. Sal placed his eyes in the rearview mirror, watching until the woman's form became no larger than an insect. It was the first human he'd seen in two days. Damn cowards, he thought, all of us.

He opened the center console and pulled from the pile of junk, a hand-rolled cigarette. They tasted like shit, but hey—when times are tough—anything to fill that void. The smoke curled like a snake out the corner of his mouth and freed itself into the atmosphere by means of the car window. It felt so good to get that nicotine flowing, but it burnt so bad. He liked to smoke even if it was detrimental to his health and the environment, but knew he should quit. No smoker is ignorant to the fact that smoking is bad, he thought. They just enjoy the rituals.

By the time he reached the grocery store, he'd seen four more people. Each had exhibited the same behavior as the first, utter surprise at a moving vehicle and choppy lethargic movements. The grocery store parking lot had only ten cars scattered about, all at various distances. None were clustered together, almost like the drivers had been fearful of any other mechanical object, and thus parked a distance away. It was weird to see it like that, Sal thought, with no carts floating about, with no moms pushing kids in strollers.

He pulled into a front row spot and threw the car into park. The front doors were policed by an officer of the law, holding an assault rifle at ready. Sal had never seen an assault rifle, but recognized the weapon from the endless number of action movies he'd watched. It was times like those that he figured he should have gone into a different field, maybe one where you learn to use weapons.

The officer nodded through his dark swat mask at Sal. Apparently the pudgy man didn't pose a threat, and Sal nodded courteously back. One of the reasons he knew it wasn't possible for him to fare well in the army or police force was his distaste for authority. The higher-ups always telling you what to do—and what else are they but people? No more important in life than your waiter or your bellhop.

Sal picked out a red and green pepper, a few potatoes, and moved on. The produce looked like shit, but again, when times are tough. He grabbed milk, eggs, and bread. He also chucked a box of cereal in the cart, high in fiber. Have to watch the cholesterol, he thought.

The sole cashier was withered and blue-skinned—her wrinkles folding over themselves and enveloping her forehead. Her white hair was patchy and her scalp looked like the hide of a flea-ridden mutt. He'd never seen her working there. Sal tossed his items on the black conveyor belt and placed a wooden separator behind them. The old woman made eye contact, and then quickly looked down as she scanned the items individually.

As his groceries swam down the belt, Sal moved forward with them. He pulled his shopper's card out, dangling from his keys, and presented it to the woman.

"Hi, Sal…" she croaked, holding out a shriveled palm to accept his keys.

Sal looked up. He wondered how she knew his name. Had it generated on his card? Then, he looked at her name tag and nearly fainted. It read "June." She was the thirty-three-year-old cashier, with whom he had so often conversed in the past.

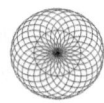

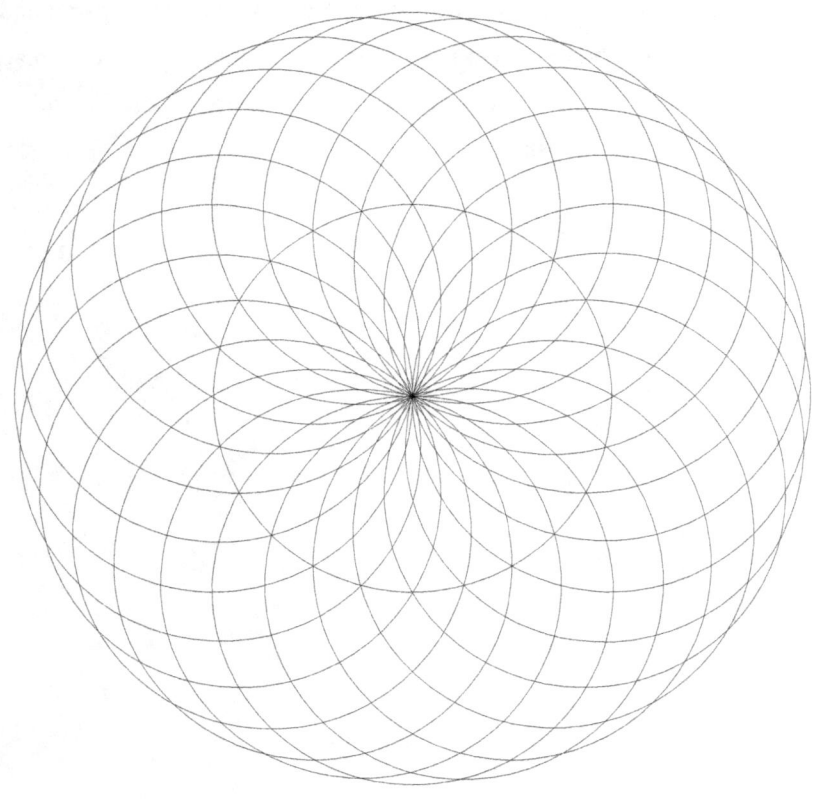

Chapter 13

SENSE OF SECURITY

It was a twenty-minute drive to Madrid, and upon arriving, they were quick to realize that the airport was more than congested. It was packed tight as a can of sardines. The people were acting like scared gazelle, fleeing the pursuing lion, in flight of an unavoidable enemy.

They learned that the machines had started to pop up everywhere; even the calm and collected began to slacken in their composure. Behind Marco's strong exterior, he was shaken. He had only shown Sheila this vulnerability and felt bad about lying to Manuel. He told his boss that his mother had taken seriously ill, but Manuel gave Marco a knowing smile and told him to "Take your time."

Manuel always understood, and Marco wondered how he did it. In the age of ignorance and lack of manners, it's tough to stay on the same page as any one person, including those to whom you're close.

The traffic was backed up past the parking gate. It was a slow process, full of honks and yells, middle fingers, but eventually their sedan was let through. Parking was another thing altogether. They drove around—Sheila's sandaled feet on the dashboard, head lolled into her headrest—before finally coming into a spot at the back of the lot.

A family four-pack was unloading their station wagon and the mother rushed them in hurried Spanish. "Vamanos, vamanos! *We're going to miss the plane.*"

Marco wondered what they were trying to escape. Or had they not heard the news? If these obscurities were all over the globe, then surely they must have known. He considered the family to be like himself. At first, he believed a safe haven existed. However, upon learning more about the situation, he wanted to see his family in case it truly was the end of days, to be with those you loved.

The small boy, who Marco typecast as the son, carried only a small backpack. Were there toys or clothing in there, Marco couldn't tell. Either way, the boy looked unconcerned with the need to rush things. The small boy's slowly swinging arms and unperturbed face said "If it's my time, then so be it."

Then, the family disappeared into the entrance. Before the small boy could follow, he checked over his shoulder, as if he felt the eyes of an unknown watching him. Marco looked away.

"Ready?" he asked Sheila.

She pulled her feet off the dashboard and rolled her neck. "Yeah, I suppose." Then, she gathered her brown locks into a tight knot on top of her head.

Marco locked the door thrice, checked all of the doors, and then popped the trunk with the automatic opener. Each of them had packed a week's worth of clothing into the three-foot piece of Samsonite. Marco lugged the bag from the trunk and opened the guide. No sense in wasting your energy. He hoped they'd brought enough stuff.

Sheila led Marco with her body. He watched as she prowled into the airport lobby, right past the security guards, who just so happened to be carrying large guns. They stopped him.

"Sir," the gorilla-sized one said, "We're going to need to check your bag."

Marco obliged and unzipped the bag. The behemoth rifled through their clothes and cleared them for passage. Sheila stood beyond the threshold, impatiently tilting her head in the anything-but-pleased way she always did.

"I'm surprised they didn't strip search you… fuckin' assholes."

Marco loved Sheila's sass, but only when it was directed elsewhere. It could be harsh, but when not on the receiving end, always humorous.

"If they were smart they would have strip searched you," Marco said. He put his arm around her waist and walked alongside her.

They stopped short once noticing that all the lines for United States airlines were absent. U.S. Airways, Delta, and American Airlines booths all had their lights turned off.

"I'll be back," Marco said.

"Where are you going?"

"To find out what's happening. Just watch our bag."

Marco rushed to customer service. There was a short line, but it was fast moving. Families bustled about with screaming babies and ranting parents. Hurried voices of frantic, desperate people filled the station with a ruckus of epic proportions. The small woman behind the desk was quite pretty, even beautiful, with her hair pulled up in a tight, black ponytail. Marco read her name tag: "Celestina."

"Buenos Tardes, Senor!" She smiled a very white smile at him. "Le puedo ayudar?" *How can I help you?*

"*I need a flight to New York, but all of the airlines to America are closed. Do you know when they'll reopen?*"

"*I apologize, sir, for the inconvenience. The United States borders are temporarily closed to civilian traffic.*"

"*For how long?*"

"*There is no set amount of time, sir. They have declared a state of National Emergency. I'm sure that once the situation—*"

Marco stormed off, uncaring of how he was perceived. The farther he moved, he did feel bad, though, for not allowing Celestina to rationalize. Yet, what was rational any longer? Giant machines from the ground certainly weren't. Even Marco's behavior had been irrational. He never should have wandered into the forest in the middle of the night. What do survivalists use? They use the buddy system. If he had tripped and cut his wrist or banged his head, he could have lain dead and nobody would have known what had happened to him.

"I can't believe we're headed back. It was such a long trip." Sheila's feet were on the dashboard again. Marco always told her to take them down in case of an accident, but she said her trust in his driving overshadowed the chances. He knew himself to be a good driver, but it was the other reclusive maniacs that were unpredictable, whom he did not trust.

"I told you that you didn't have to come if you didn't want to."

"So you *would* have just left me by myself? That's real nice."

The traffic was steady. A blue Nissan cut them off without a blinker. Just the type of mishap Marco was thinking of—where the idiot assumes you're watching them, instead of the road—the fucking Earnhardt wannabes.

"I wouldn't have left you, obviously." He said it just to dig at her. Marco laid on the horn. "Can you please take your feet down?"

For once she listened, something that didn't happen very often. Her headiness usually commanded her actions.

Outside of Madrid, the traffic had come to a standstill for nearly an hour. Sheila cranked on a Nickelback album and listened to it clean through. It wasn't his favorite band, but it kept a smile on her face and was better than most of the shit on the radio.

"What if we have to pass one of the machines?" Sheila asked.

"I'm sure they would have the road blocked if it was too close. Don't you think—a barricade or something?"

"But what is too close?"

It boggled Marco. If there were any nuclear emissions, the result wouldn't necessarily be immediate. It could tax their respiratory system years down the road, mutate into cancer. He remembered watching a show on the History Channel about the nuclear testing in Nevada in the 60's. These people had sat in lawn chairs watching the atom bombs like they were fireworks—cheering, unaware of the fallout floating over their heads, which was floating into their lungs. They hadn't known the effects, just as nobody knew the true nature of the machines.

"That's why I said we should get away. Nobody knows anything. They can't get close to the things to test them and there is no communication. So we're pretty much in the dark."

"Do you think it's like this everywhere? America has all that spruced up technology."

"I don't know. I had hoped so, but it isn't looking good. Why would America close their doors, if they were doing just fine?"

He hadn't realized before, just how much Sheila depended on him for reassurance. She thought he was well informed. Maybe America was better, but maybe it was worse. It could be a shut-out, he thought. He wished he had all the answers, but then again, would it be better or worse? Is it better to know the harsh truth, or to live on in blissful ignorance?

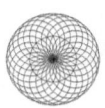

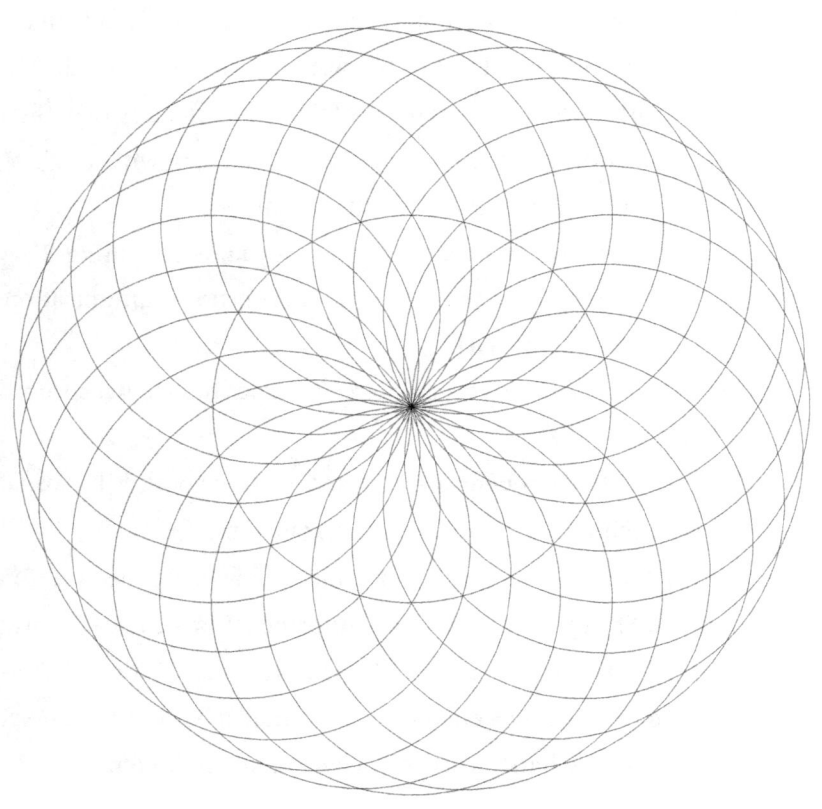

Chapter 14

THE COUNTRY
OF THE DEAD

When they pulled into the black, rock-covered driveway, Marco saw that the garage door hung open. He couldn't call his uncle to let him know they were coming, but assumed his uncle to be at home. Uncle Ricky was a fisherman and worked on his own hours, which amounted to close to never.

For the most part Uncle Ricky, short for Ricardo, lived off of his land. He grew all sorts of garden veggies in his backyard and thrived on seafood seven nights a week. Uncle Ricky had earned the downtime. He had worked tirelessly to pay off the small house—now only paying for electricity, and using water he pulled from his well.

What work he missed outside of home, he made up for by either doing yard work or carpentry. Before Marco and Sheila had left his house the last time, Uncle Ricky constructed a fifteen-foot shed in a span of three days. Marco liked to think of his father's brother as resourceful.

From the garage an electric whine escaped, the sound of a circular saw cutting timber. The man was at it again. This time, Marco thought, maybe he was building a fallout shelter. It wouldn't have been beyond all belief, and it was certainly within his boundaries to do so.

Ricky was bent over a saw horse that was holding a two-by-four. He cut it into shorter lengths in perfect lines. The man didn't wear goggles—he claimed they were for pussies—and his only safety precaution was to watch your fingers. His face was strained beneath his hearty black beard, but upon noticing Marco and Sheila, it changed immediately to inquisitive.

"Marco, Sheila? What are you doing back here? Not that I am unhappy to see you… but you just left!"

Marco dove into his open arms, a big bear of a man, and felt his powerful love. He marveled at the older man's inability to waver in the current situation.

"I came to see if you'd heard from Mom."

Ricky released him and Marco felt the air squeeze back into his lungs. "Our phone, radio, and television were all down by the second day we got home from vacation."

"Unfortunately mine is down as well, but I did have the chance to speak with your mother before it happened. She was fine then, said the closest machine popped into Nelson's Corner Store."

"How far from Nelson's?" Marco asked.

Ricky lowered his gaze sarcastically and frowned. "Right into the middle."

"Was—"

Uncle Ricky nodded his head and closed his eyes, as if sending a silent, but well-needed prayer. He reopened his eyes, again the jovial uncle, only willing to showcase his vulnerability in small spurts. Mr. Nelson had been to Ricky, what Manuel was to Marco—a boss, yet, a valuable friend and mentor. He'd spent his first four years of adulthood as a Spanish infantryman. When Marco's parents decided they were moving to the states (Marco was eight), naturally Uncle Ricky decided it not such a bad idea to follow. He left the service and moved to America. Marco grew to adore Ricky, but was devastated when seven years later, his favorite uncle decided to immigrate back to the home country. From then on, Marco only saw Uncle Ricky on the spare summer trips to Spain.

It was in those seven years that Mr. Nelson had taken Uncle Ricky under his wing as a store clerk, eventually assistant manager, and formed a tight bond. When Ricky returned to Spain, Mr. Nelson talked to him on the phone almost every day. He made a point of spewing any and all information to Marco, of his uncle's well-being. Marco spoke with him periodically on the phone, but after long, it became far less frequent. Until, eventually Marco only spoke with his uncle on holidays and birthdays. However, Marco always held a very special spot in his heart for those times when Ricky reappeared.

Marco changed the subject. "What's it you're making now?"

"Some folks down the road are throwing their daughter's wedding. They know my work, so they asked me to build an arbor."

"I do, too. It's very meticulous," Sheila said. "I love our bed frame."

Ricky blushed. "Thanks, Sheila. They paid me five hundred bucks up front."

Those were the jobs Ricky paid his house with—the odd jobs and freelance carpentry. Marco didn't know where he had learned the skills, but figured his uncle to have picked them up along the way. At first appearance, Ricky was a big, dumb behemoth. The truth is Uncle Ricardo was one of the smartest men Marco had ever known. He could dissect mathematical problems with little thought and when given logical equations, he could answer in seconds.

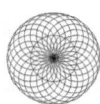

"**W**hy don't I make us all a little dinner from the garden? No?"

"Actually, Uncle Ricky, I think we're going to have to pass."

Uncle Ricky frowned. "Why is that?"

"We're going to try and find a boat or small—"Sheila slapped Marco's arm and gave him a death stare through serious brown eyes. "Of course we'll stay for dinner," she said.

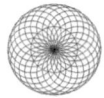

Ricky had served up a wealth of seafood tapas, as well as a garden salad with homemade balsamic dressing, mushrooms, and bell peppers. It was very good eating, and it satisfied Marco's stomach, eased his anxiety. With it came a level of comfort he had not felt in a good week. To him it felt like the Earth had come loose of its axis, and was off spinning in outer space.

Marco followed his uncle out past the shed he had built, past the chrysanthemums—yet, another of his uncle's talents being gardening—and walked along the dock. The dock sat worn, hanging over the ocean. Waves splashed against the supports, but the platform held strong.

Ricky offered Marco a cigar. "Best around," his uncle said.

"I don't usually smoke, only during celebrations."

"And this isn't a celebration?"

"You know what I mean, uncle. If a baby is born, if my friend had a promotion, then we would smoke cigars—at a wedding."

Uncle Ricky cut a quarter of an inch off the mouth of one cigar. He handed the circumcised smoke to his nephew. Then, he cut the tip of his own and lit a match, held it out for Marco to light his. Marco pushed the dime-sized end into the orange flame.

"I would call life a celebration."

Marco sucked the smoke into his mouth using his tongue, puffed it out over the water. "Yeah… it could be worse."

Uncle Ricky stood solid near the edge of the dock, close enough for any other person to fall right into the fierce ocean. His cheeks puffed from the inhalation, and his eyes regarded the water.

"Do you know why they call this place Finisterre?"

"Yeah... why?"

"The Romans discovered it. They felt it was the farthest point on Earth, or literally the end of the world."

Marco held his cigar between two fingers. "Our Columbus proved them wrong."

"Fuck, Columbus," Ricky said. "The Romans believed the end of the world was where the country of the dead began..." he hesitated, puffing. "I know I seem tough, but I don't like this, Marco. I can feel the world *changing*, and not for the better. We've done so much damage to this planet, it almost seems irreversible."

Marco took a deep breath of the salted air. He took in the sincerity of the Costa da Morte, the intrinsic beauty. How in a blink it could disappear.

"Back in my days, sixties and seventies, people used to stand up for what they believed in. Now they just lie there ranting at the television."

"We need action," Marco said.

Ricky turned, flicked the head off of his cigar. "Damn straight, or we may as well jump right off this dock—join that country that's already jam-packed."

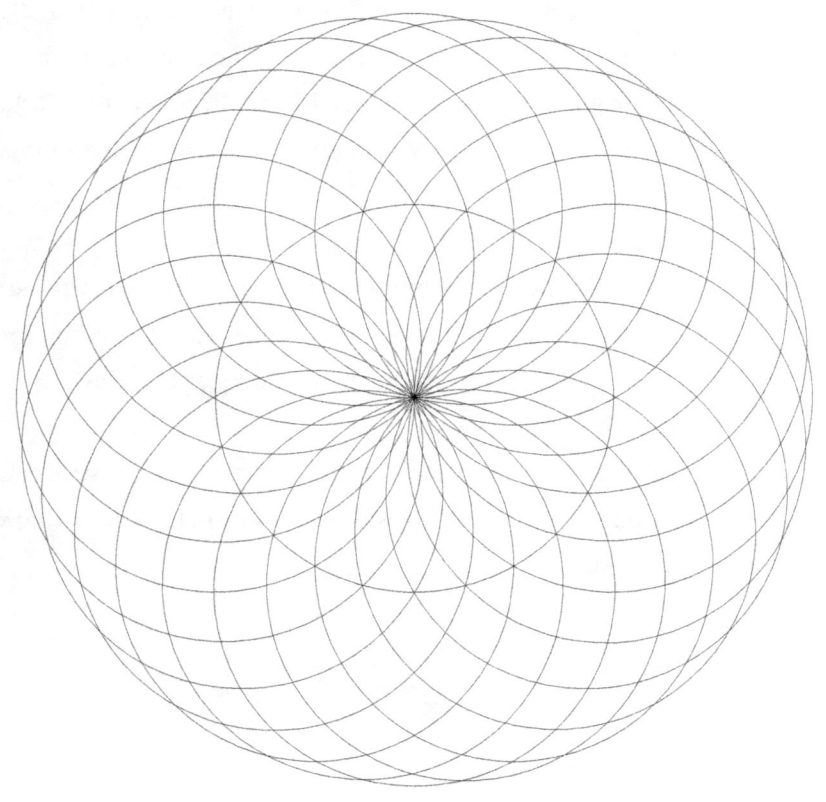

Chapter 15

THE START OF UPHEAVAL

"The engines won't turn back on," Pete told Captain Portis. "Should we start to ready the lifeboats yet?"

The sky had deepened to a dark shade of blue and the wind had graduated to a solid rush. It knocked against the windows on the bridge and skittered debris across the deck like leaves in autumn.

"Not yet. We need to distract the passengers."

"We could move them off the deck, away from the sides."

Portis volunteered Mary. "She needs to figure something out. She is in charge of passenger fare. If we rush them off deck it will alarm them."

The sea bounced the cruise ship like a baby on a knee, and Portis actually stumbled from the motion. He caught his balance and took a seat in the chair next to Pete. "Do you think this has anything to do with the Bermuda Triangle?" the captain asked. Pete checked the coordinates on the electronic mapping system, which was frozen, as if he hadn't already memorized their position. Good thing he had, for it was no longer working. The Triangle was obviously mysterious and feared in the cruise ship line of business. Portis remembered Pete making mention of the fact when they entered it—as was typically the case—something along the lines of, "Oooh… and we've entered the Triangle! Pit of Poseidon!"

Was it foreshadowing, he wondered, or just a poor coincidence? Either way, it supremely unnerved the captain. He was a man of reason, but also, a man who loved to study the metaphysical and superstitious. Since a boy, he had been not only fascinated with the natural, but also with the supernatural. The conspiracies, if you will.

The lights blinked off on the dashboard of the ship's controls and Pete focused his taut face on the captain. He spoke imperatively. "Captain, I think it's about time for those life rafts."

Portis stood and looked through the navigational windows, over the deck. The crowd was growing at the front of the ship. He could vaguely make out the form of Mary, bustling about in her skirt and blouse, eager to please and hopeful to not disappoint. Select passengers waved their hands at her and some looked as though they were yelling. It wasn't fair of her to take the brunt of the abuse.

"No life rafts."

Pete stood next to Portis. "What do you mean no life rafts?"

Portis turned solemnly, looked Pete directly in the eyes. "Do you not feel the power of these waves? They would eat those tiny flotation devices alive. It would be reckless of us to deploy them, containing live people. We'd be murderers."

Pete threw his hands up in defense, his eyes became angry. "We can't just sit and wait, sir!"

Portis straightened his collar and fluffed his white suit for wrinkles. "It's all we can do, my friend. I'm going to try and diffuse this deck situation. You continue with the phones and VHF."

Pete sighed and sat back down, and immediately tried the phone again.

Portis walked out of the cockpit with his head held high. He knew there was potential for disaster aboard, possibly even violence, but he was prepared. It was his job to be ready for situations like it. As he closed the door to the cockpit, he heard the phone slam onto the cradle and a very frustrated man yell "Damn it!"

Mary screamed "All right everyone... just back away from the railing!" She tried to force her way through the crowd to the very tip of the bow, but she couldn't break the ranks. She slid her arm through a man and a woman, trying to pry them apart. "*Excuse* me."

The man turned on her. He wore dark sunglasses and a light blue polo. Everything from his tight haircut to his toned body said East L.A. douche bag. The woman said "Hey!", and the man came to her defense.

"Stop shoving, lady! And where the fuck do you get off telling us what to do. I don't see a fucking badge. Why don't you just *back* off?"

A few droplets of spit rained onto Mary's tanned cheek and she wiped them off, as fast as she would if they contained the plague. His shoulder closed her off. She stood there not knowing what to do. She could not commandeer the situation, regardless of her actions—she just didn't have the authority.

The ship dropped with a wave and the crowd "Ooohed!" in concert. Mary didn't like the feel of the ocean. She had travelled many a cruise, weathered many a storm aboard the massive vessels. None of it felt natural to her. Sure, storms crashed waves against ships, hurricanes had sank them in the past, but it was not the same. There was a different aura about it. She could feel it like a force field, holding them all hostages. Being in charge of everyone's well-being was already a difficult task. Taking care of your own life was even harder.

Mary strolled out of the crowd and kept her eye on the douche in the tight polo. She hated the type of person he was, and she didn't even need to know him to understand his entire persona. It was sad to think that people who were so shallow, their exterior couldn't hide their inner complex, existed on the sphere of a planet. She knew countless of the sort, the popular ones in school, who always thought they were ahead of the curve in the game of life, but came to find out after college that wasting their time worrying about others' perceptions of you actually stunted growth in your wisdom. It wasn't worth her time to allow any more of her attention to be assuaged by the loser.

Yet, her mind wouldn't escape the confrontation. It stuck like a post-it note to her brain. She had dated the type too often. They were Mister Cool in public, treating you like a princess, but in private they had the Mister Hyde going on. They would treat you like a dog. One guy had even hit her. Luckily, she was strong enough to walk away, unlike so many women who allow the behavior to escalate. Mary needed a good man, like Captain Portis. He would take care of her.

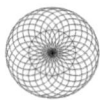

The keys of the two cops dangled, clanging off of their belts. It was about time for order. The crowd was increasing tenfold by the minute, passengers catching drift of the news and being too curious for their own good. Any second the situation could escalate past a point of reason, and then they would be in some real trouble. Some of the passengers were already becoming agitated by the lack of answers, but Portis knew it best to keep them in the cold. The less they knew, the less there was for them to panic over.

They walked through the crowd, the cops leading by force. "Make an example of him," Portis ordered.

The first cop tapped the man on the shoulder. "Hey, buddy."

The jerk turned around—pointed hair at his widow's peak, dark sunglasses (a tool)—and asked "*What*?"

"Sir, I'm going to ask you to come with us, please."

The guy's face shrank into his head as if it was the most preposterous thing he had heard in his entire life. He laughed in the deck officer's face, surely his breath smelt of Altoids over beer.

"You gotta' be fucking kidding me. Hon' did you hear this guy?"

He turned to talk to his girlfriend and the cop made a move. Twisting the agitator's arm behind his back, he said "C'mon, buddy."

He started to drag the loudmouth away, much to the displeasure of his girlfriend.

She swung her small, black purse at the officer's head. "Get off of him, dickhead!"

Cop number two came to defense, holding the small wiry woman back. Portis saw the situation going one of two ways, and it was exactly his prediction. No matter which party was in the wrong, the masses tend to side with the civilians.

"Hey, lay off!" somebody shouted.

Another woman shouted, "What are you doing to him!"

Civil unrest was at hand, and where had Mary gone? Portis came to save her, to put to justice the man who had disrespected her, and she disappeared. The captain searched the faces of the passengers for a sign of recognition, the slight wrinkles at the corners of her mouth just beginning to form, or the small mole on her upper lip. What finally commanded his attention was her fiery head of hair. It was turned down and he figured her to be crying.

He shoved through the crowd to try and get at her, but frustrated passengers continually stole his attention.

"Hey, Captain! What's going on? Are we going to be moving anytime soon?" Sometimes it was even hard for Portis to keep a level head, with all the idiots around.

"Hey, Captain..." the guy said grabbing Portis by the sleeve. It was becoming too physical. "I'm talking to you."

The man was around forty-five with a greying head of curls. He wore a salt and pepper goatee and stood a measly five-foot-six. Portis didn't react like the man had hoped. "Sir... kindly remove your hand from my jacket."

"Not until you start giving some answers, buddy. I've been standing out here for an hour and a half in the cold."

For some reason Portis didn't see that as his problem. He hadn't told all the people to wait on deck for answers. It wasn't like somebody had indicated to him that a giant spinning spire would break free of the ocean. Just as the passengers, he was out in the cold. The man could have gone into his warm cabin at any point in time.

"Things are perfectly well under control…"

The man let go of Portis's sleeve and grabbed him by the lapels. "You listen here. I have two teenage daughters up in our cabin that I love more than the world, you better start being truthful."

Portis could see the cops struggling, as more people were joining in on the fight for Mister Polo, yelling and pushing. The black cop was still being beaten by the man's girlfriend. Portis figured it was just a matter of time before a weapon was extracted. The crowd's voice rose as one, much like the waves of the ocean.

"Okay," Portis said. "Just let go of me."

The paunchy middle-aged man let the fabric unwrinkled from his grip.

"The situation at hand will hopefully get no worse. In the meantime, I have ordered the kitchen staff to cook a nice roast dinner. I suggest you take your daughters and enjoy a hot meal. I'm not sure how much longer the power will be on. Still, there is no cause for panic just yet."

"No cause for panic? We all see that thing out there. It ain't normal. Why don't you just turn this damn ship around? Get us all back home… I don't want to die out here."

Portis started to get flustered. He was trying to be as professional as possible, but then, he was only human. He poked the smaller man in the chest hard. "Lower your fucking voice. You want to live, then cooperate. I only know as much as you do."

He admitted, "I'm only a sea captain."

Chapter 16

PARANOIA

Two young girls played outside—a rarity of the age, especially considering the circumstances. They wore cotton shorts and white tees even though it was fifty degrees outside. The temperature was dropping rapidly, Sal could feel it. Fifty degrees in Southern California was uncommon in the daytime, even in the winter months. It was a place of warmth, regardless of the time of year.

He ripped down the Pacific Coast Highway, away from the grocery. The people outside were few and far between, but those who were outside grabbed Sal's attention more than fluorescent clothing or a hot air balloon. Speed limits were unimportant to him, (not that they had ever regulated him before) and on the merge toward Park Avenue he almost collided with another car.

Sal shrank away from his door as the red Honda Accord laid its horn down. He was supposed to yield, but assumed his was the only car on the road. He realized it was a truly silly thought. Things were bad, but not quite that bad. People were still leaving the house, just with less frequency. They went to work and came home, no errands or trips. His area of town had always been a fairly quiet one, anyway. So it was simple to assume there would be no cars outside.

The other driver ripped away at the next stoplight, taking a left.

When he finally made it home, it was much to his surprise to see

Norman Blanchett. Sal never liked Norman, even though he'd never talked to him. The man stood in his front yard, watching *everything*. He would stare at your car until you stepped from it, and would then follow you with his eyes until you were safely inside your home. If you stopped and stared back, he accepted your challenge.

Sal pretended to fiddle with an object in his console, hoping that Norman would go inside. He glanced in the rearview mirror, just long enough to catch a snapshot of Norman in his dark blue windbreaker. The lower half of his body was hidden by his car, and his hands were jammed into the pockets on the torso part of the jacket. Sal could not see his eyes, only the light reflecting off the glass of his spectacles. Of course, Mister Blanchett's head was aimed directly at Sal's driveway.

"Look away, you fuck," Sal wished in the sanctity of his car.

He slammed the glove box closed and snagged the grocery bag from the passenger's seat. Doing his best not to give Norman his attention, he shuffled around his car, fumbling for the keys in his pocket. It was important to minimize the amount of time Norman would be watching him, but dropping the keys didn't help. When he bent to pick them up, he instinctively peeked at Norman.

The neighbor across the street had his head turned down, staring at Sal. His head of white hair was always set in a perfect comb-over. Sal thought he looked like a bobble-head in that position. He wanted to knock the man's head back so it would bounce.

Sal turned and walked up the path to his front door. "Nosy little pudgy fuck," he said to himself under his breath. Then, he turned the key in the lock and entered his house, which was much warmer and private.

Norman Blanchett wasn't outside since the machines had emerged. Sal had been keeping his eye on the neighborhood, a bit paranoid he knew, but in such dire situations, one had to be. He remembered watching the riots in South Central Los Angeles on TV, seeing houses and businesses raided for no reason. It was a time for paranoia. Lack thereof could prove deadly.

However, Norman had always been the neighborhood watch dog. Sometimes Sal would refer to him as Mr. Nosy, because whether you were doing yard work or grilling out, Norman would be watching you from his pocketed stance or sitting in a lawn chair. It was bittersweet. Sal felt the neighborhood was safer that way, but it also made him feel uncomfortable at times.

Sal checked on Norman. He was still out there, no longer looking at Sal's house, which he had been doing for the past forty-five minutes, but gazing off down the street. The neighbor rolled on his heels, as he did quite often. To Sal, Blanchett's behavior spoke of boredom, of a lonely life with nothing better to do than watch other folk, pry into their business. Then, he caught himself doing exactly the same.

Somewhere along the line it had become a world of nosiness. Sal couldn't remember growing up with all the celebrity rags they have nowadays. He often caught snippets of celeb shows and felt disgusted by them. As if being poor wasn't enough for some people, they had to flood their lives with an ever-present reminder of the lavish lifestyles and popularity of which they would never be endowed.

For Sal, money was easy. Working for Sanz and Peters (the number one accounting firm in Southern California) definitely had its benefits—one of them being a seven figure income. He threw cash into the wind but couldn't care less. His father had taught him the value "You can't bring it with you!" along with the notion to not let people walk all over you, and to also not care what others thought of you. It was a deadly combination, which had propelled his career exponentially.

It wasn't that Sal cared what Blanchett thought about him, he just didn't *want* to be watched. For all of the money in the world Sal would give to have those beady eyes mind their own Goddamn business for one day.

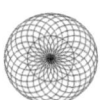

Chapter 17

DEPARTED

"Come back if you need anything else," Uncle Ricky said, holding Marco's shoulders in his bear paws. "Anything at all, I'm more than happy to help."

"I know you are, uncle."

Ricky pulled Marco into his body. "Take care of Sheila," he whispered. "She's a good woman."

"I always do," Marco said. "Take care of yourself."

Ricky let go of his nephew and took a large step back. His eyes asked if Marco was being honest, and his lips were puckered as if to say "Seriously?" Then, he opened his arms to Sheila, who practically ran into them.

"Mi amor," he said, kissing her on both cheeks. He also whispered into her ear, his head bobbing as he spoke quickly.

Her head rolled back in laughter and she said, "Okay."

"Bye, uncle," Marco said getting into the car. Sheila gave a backwards wave. She slid into the passenger's seat and kicked her legs onto the dashboard with a sigh.

"What did he say to you?"

"He told me to watch over you, because you're headstrong."

"That's it?"

"Yeah."

"So? What's so funny about that? I take it as a compliment."

She winked at him with a smile. "You can be cocky sometimes."

Marco ignited the engine and cranked the heat up. Despite it being the middle of September, the thermometer in the car read forty-eight degrees, blistering cold for Northern Spain. The night was coming on and with it the drought of warmth, subtly reminiscent of the night his father had passed away.

He was seventeen and he fell asleep early with the window open, a calm breeze elongating the whispers in the trees to a whistle. Out of nowhere he was awoken by the sound of unforgettable crying, it was full of despair and utter disbelief. Marco had sat up in bed, thinking his mother was hurt. He practically ran out of his bedroom, nearly tripping over his mother's defeated body. She sat with her back to the wall, her feet pressed against the opposite side of the hallway. Marco thought of it as a screeching cry, uncontrollable and honest. Her entire body was limp. Her arms were loose, legs were like spaghetti, and even her shoulders had lost her typical composure.

"Mother, what's wrong?" he asked.

She never answered. The only thing she did was to sit and rack in helpless sobs. Marco remembered crouching and putting his arm over her shoulders. She wouldn't make eye contact, just stared into nothingness as if lost in space. When he heard the sirens, he somehow just *knew*. His body lost all of its heat and he fell into a trance, hugging his mother like he was a belt, trying to find some comfort for either of them. There was only distance.

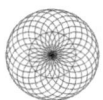

Uncle Ricky's old friend was the captain of the export ship Brutania. It was mainly a boat to send olives, spices, and fish, but Ricky had claimed that on occasion it sent people. En route to the shipyard they encountered a road block. Cars were locked on the highway to a complete halt. On the opposing side of the barrier, cars sped by and even a man on a bicycle, covered in sweat and wearing a look of utter fear.

"What now?" Sheila asked.

"Must be an accident." He flipped on Radio Nacional de Espana, Spanish Public Radio. The speakers to the car whined an excruciatingly high pitch. Sheila covered her ears and fell into a hunched over position.

"Turn it off, turn it off!" she yelled.

Marco winced from the sound, which felt like it was permeating his brain. His hand shook violently as he reached for the dial. Finally, he gripped and tore it to the left. The radio clicked off.

"We have to be near one of them," Marco said.

"Ya' think?"

It lingered in Marco's eardrum, a constant reminder of the threat to the natural world. His ear rang, the type which was supposed to mean that somebody a long way off was thinking of you, and Marco wondered if the machines were targeting him. He felt they were speaking to him, telling him to turn around and go back home, look after Manuel and the café.

"I wish I knew exactly where these things are so that we could avoid them."

Marco fell to inspection of Sheila's face. She wore an expression of carelessness. As long as he didn't turn the radio back on, she wouldn't care one way or another whether or not they drove around, or directly through, the obscure machines. She was content with being along for the ride and never participating in the decision-making aspect.

Sheila looked at him. "We could get off. Then, in little spurts try the radio. We'll turn it down quickly if it squeaks."

"*Squeaks*," she said. Marco thought it was a funny word to use.

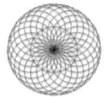

He was thinking of survival and decided that hands make for good tools. If the world were to come to an end, he was sure to be one of the few to last. Darwin had called it survival of the fittest. What classified as fit? The most physically developed specimen or that with the right ratio of clever calculation and ingenuity? Ricky had hands for tools and he knew how to use them; Marco was more of a calculator with spare dexterity.

He liked to think that Sheila would make it, but he had a feeling it would be of his own recourse. For most, he realized, it would unfortunately come to that fate. Without the ease of grocery stores or the gas pump, reliant humans would fall to defeat, especially in America. In other countries, like Spain, food was local and fresh. Everything in America was imported or *created*. The food was filled with shit. The thought made him worry for his mother.

With the cease of immigration, would importation stop as well? Would his mother go to the grocery store only to find the produce shelves bare? The international items would be absent, and the only food in the store would be genetically modified crap, containing trace amounts of any nutritional value. Being a Spaniard he knew at least one thing—good food leads to a good and long life.

Sheila flipped the radio on. There was a slight whistle, but not paining. Marco felt like some voice was going to say "This is only a test."

"Are we almost there?" Marco asked. He looked over his right shoulder, and seeing an opening moved into the lane. The road was still congested, but there was room to move.

Sheila looked over the map. "It looks it."

Using her thumb and forefinger she gauged the distance. "Probably about twenty more miles."

"Why don't you put a CD in?"

Sheila opened the glove box and took from it a hard black square. It cracked open and she flipped through. "It's not like we haven't listened to them all a thousand times. Anything particular you're in the mood for?"

"Something… anything."

Sheila put the CD's in her lap and clapped. She smiled. "What a decision!"

Marco shook his head. "I really don't care. Just anything to take my mind away. Except for the Beatles."

"You don't hate the Beatles… you just pretend to."

Sheila placed a disc at the mouth of the CD player and the slot gobbled it up. It was some pop rock band. Marco wasn't sure which, most of them tended to sound in a similar realm to him. He was glad the CD source was uninterrupted. There's nothing to drag a long car ride on than lack of music.

After listening to half the record, they saw the rows of docks lining the ocean shore. Marco was excited to be there, despite the transatlantic trip they would need to endure.

"We have Dramamine left, right?" he asked.

Sheila dug through the console once more, through pay stubs, napkins, and boxes of emergency meds. She pulled out a small yellow box and handed a pill to him.

"I'm scared, Marco," she admitted.

He wanted to second her notion, just so that she wouldn't feel like a baby, but couldn't. He knew it was not smart to plead insecurity when you are meant to be the stable one. It was his time to feign confidence.

"I know," he said. He rubbed her thigh just above the knee. "Believe me… it's what we should be doing, though."

"What if we get caught?"

All the while, he thought she was scared of what the machines could be doing to the Earth, what could happen on the open ocean. There was so much more to worry over than being caught by the authorities. He had to snicker.

"I don't think we'll get caught, honey. Ricky wouldn't endanger us."

Sheila's face shouted doubt. "That's why he's been arrested five times? Because he is a staunch rule follower."

"He was an activist."

They stopped talking once they reached the gates to the shipping facility. Outside the gates, two guards stood with rifles. They were clad in camouflage and were routinely turning cars away, panting and yelling. Directly ahead of their car was a blue sedan. When it reached the gates, it idled. As per usual, one of the guards approached the car window.

The exhaust from its tailpipe dusted their windshield. Marco waited for it to "*Bang!*" like Uncle Buck's. The guard leaned into the car window with his hands on the top of the car. Marco could see the shadow of the man in the driver's seat, rummaging. Then, the shadow moved swiftly, just a flash of dark. The guard at his post raised his rifle.

"Oh, my God… what's happening?" Sheila worried.

The identifier at the car window stepped back, holding his neck. The thick gash across his throat bled profusely. The sedan kicked into drive and rammed the legs of the uninjured guard, while simultaneously his rifle fired.

Sheila covered her eyes, screaming, and Marco's heart raced. The car was still on, revving and pressing the guard into the gate. The man, whose throat was cut, fell back onto the grass. From a booth behind the gate another man rushed, brandishing a pistol.

He fired twice into the blue sedan. Marco saw shadowy spurts flutter against the windshield. The man who wore a red beret reached into the car and turned the car in reverse. When the vehicle moved enough so that the legs of the crushed were free, he cut the engine. The crushed man yelped in pain and crumbled against the wrought iron gate.

The toll-booth man lit a smoke and walked carefully toward their car. The pistol pointed at the ground. Sheila grabbed Marco by the arm. "Do something, honey."

Marco didn't want to be hasty. Obviously, the man didn't mean to harm them. He rolled his window down and waited for the guard to bend over.

"*What is your business?*"

"*We're supposed to meet Captain Rafael here,*" Marco said.

The man held the cigarette beneath his thick black mustache with two puffy chapped lips. "*Marco?*"

Marco nodded.

"*Drive in.*"

With relief, Marco shifted into drive and pulled around the blue sedan. He tried not to look, but like a car crash, it was impossible not to stare. The driver's head was blown apart, and what was left looked like red mashed potatoes. There was blood covering the body. One of the dead man's eyes was intact, and Marco couldn't help but feel it was staring right at him.

Sheila was shivering and looking the other direction. "Has it passed?"

The gate closed electronically behind them. "Yeah, it's all behind us."

Marco could see the guard with the fluffy mustache through the bars of the gate in the rearview mirror. He watched them drive into the facility, obviously wary of them, and then turned to regard the line of cars.

There were two large warehouses on either side of the access road, browned with age and decrepit. It had started to sprinkle, creating a slight pitter-patter off the metal roofs of the buildings. Vegetation climbed the walls, untrimmed and wild, and it made Marco wonder how often the facility was used.

At the end of the road, the cement turned into wood, and a long dock presented itself across the edge of the Atlantic. Waves crashed over the boardwalk, spitting foam through the cracks of the wood like hundreds of whales' blowholes.

"It can't be safe to go on a boat right now," Sheila said. "There must be a storm brewing."

"Brewing?" Marco laughed. "Haven't you ever seen 'Deadliest Catch'? Those crazy fuckers go out on boats ten times smaller than what we'll be on, with waves twenty feet high."

Sheila hit him for making fun of her word choice. She then took his hand in hers. "Just please don't let me go."

"I'll try. You have to treat me nicer, though."

Sheila let go of his hand and sighed. "What do you mean?"

"Ever since the day we left vacation, you've been on edge. Not your usual self."

Sheila took a glance out the window, as if for some fleeting inspiration. "I just haven't felt right. I haven't felt good about myself lately. I guess I've been taking it out on you a bit."

Her lips played with each other. "I'm sorry, honey."

Marco was almost always quick to forgive. "It's okay. I haven't either. I'm sorry if I've been strange, too."

They reached the end of the road which waylaid to an open expanse of ocean. There were four docked cargo ships. Men in skull caps bustled about onboard, pulling on ropes and carrying packages. A forklift delivered pallets of boxes onto the nearest boat by means of a cardboard-looking ramp. Some of the men stared at their car, but most continued on their tasks. At the foot of the ramp, a man stood holding a clipboard. He reviewed the item with his eyes and a black marker. Marco pulled up next to the man and opened his window.

"*Excuse me?*" he said quizzically.

The man was middle-aged with a full beard of brown and deep set eyes. He asked, "*Who are you?*"

Marco thought of asking the same but settled with, "Marco. *Ricky's nephew.*"

He shoved the clipboard under his arm, and tucked his marker into the vest pocket of his black, puffy coat. "*The Captain has been expecting you,*" he said, "*ever since your uncle called ahead on the radio*"

Then, the busy man hurried up the ramp. He returned a few moments later with a short chubby man. His jeans were ragged with holes in the knees and his shirt was stained in many different spots with grease and oil. He came to the window.

"*You can pull into the warehouse,*" he said pointing to the humongous building to the left of the car. The door hung open and plentiful amounts of product wrapped in plastic filled the building.

Marco drove into the mouth of the structure. A dark skinned man pointed frantically to the far right corner. He parked as close to the wall as possible.

"I don't like this, Marco. That guy over there is wicked sketchy. Can we trust our car here?"

Marco looked upon her with skepticism. "We're being smuggled out of the country, we're contraband now. Did you think they would look like businessmen?"

"No, but maybe not like people that would hang at strip clubs and mug you in the back alley."

Marco trusted his uncle's judgment, despite his past. Even if he dealt with underground sort of folk, Marco knew they must be the better of the bunch.

"I told you... Ricky wouldn't endanger us."

"I hope not."

They exited the car and Marco checked the doors to ensure they all had locked. The air outside the warehouse was ripe with mist, creating the scent of a recent shower. There were puddles to avoid in the gravel strip, between the warehouse and the dock, where the cargo ship waited for its final passengers. It spoke of neglect.

The captain wasn't at the foot of the ramp any longer. Marco started up the platform.

"What are you doing?"

Marco stopped. "What does it look like? C'mon."

Sheila stepped carefully onto the ramp, in a manner which suggested she just might fall through it. Mud and crud filled the veins of the metal appendage, and Sheila's face admitted disgust. "I hope the inside isn't as dirty as the outside."

The inside of the ship smelled of rust. Somewhere down the corridor from the entrance, a drop of water persisted. It didn't ease the doubts in Marco's mind. When aboard a floating vessel, the last thing you want to hear is a leak of any sort.

The high-ceilinged hall led left and right. Captain Rafael was talking to a crewman in a red beanie and a jean jacket. A jean jacket, Marco mused. He thought those had phased out with the fanny packs. The captain turned as the couple came closer, but was quick to relieve them of his attention.

They stood in the entrance to a much larger room. The room was packed with large orange, metal crates. Along the walls, black numbers were periodically painted, which Marco assumed were navigational indicators. The sound of forklifts rising and dropping pallets reverberated in the giant space.

They stood behind the captain and the red beanie guy. The captain gibbered in rapid Spanish about the importance of reducing footsteps, for time is money, and working to full potential. He delivered it in a non-guised package of reprimand.

Sheila tapped her foot impatiently. Marco was anxious to get settled in, as well, but always despised it when customers tapped their fingers or feet when waiting for their orders at work. He found it plain rude. He leaned in to her ear. "Calm down, will you?"

Her tapping stopped, but she wasn't pleased. She continued to fidget with her purse and fingers—anything to get her mind away from the *agonizing* wait.

The captain finally told the crewman to get back to work, and literally gave him a slap to the back of the head.

"*What gives?*" asked the man, angered by the gesture. The boss ignored him to regard Marco and Sheila. He was smiling this time.

"*Good afternoon! We finally meet.*" Captain Rafael held out his hand and Marco gave it a firm shake.

"*You know I don't do this for just anyone. If your uncle hadn't been due a huge favor…*" He shook his head and tsk-tsked. "*You would not be headed for America.*"

Sheila sighed and started to tap her purse. She hated it when Marco spoke solely in Spanish, leaving her to wonder what the hell was going on. She did not like to be left out of the loop.

"Porfavor, Captain… Habla Ingles?" Marco asked politely.

"Aaah—" the captain teetered his hand in the air. Then he used his finger and thumb to indicate a small amount. "Wee."

"*Come with me… I'll show you where you're staying.*"

The captain's determined steps brought them through the middle of the warehouse—passing 3B, 4A, and 4B. Marco hung back, for he knew Sheila would question their conversation. Sure enough, when the leader was out of earshot, Sheila probed Marco.

"What did he say?"

"Just that we're lucky. I guess he must have owed my uncle a favor. Otherwise, he said we never would have gotten out of the country."

"Must have been some dirty favor your uncle did for him."

"Friends do favors for each other."

Sheila laughed. "Yeah, like borrowing money, or giving them a ride."

When they stopped, Sheila said "Uh-uh."

One of the crates was open. Inside were a small cot and an oil lantern.

The bed was torn on the side and the sheets were stained with pee or poo, or blood—Marco wasn't sure.

"I am *not* sleeping or staying in a crate like a fucking animal," she said.

The captain thought this was amusing. Despite the language barrier, it was obvious the message Sheila was trying to get across.

"*There are two things...*" the captain said. "*One, you must not leave the crate until we port, unless I tell you to. Two, if you are caught—for Port Authority or the Coast Guard will inspect the ship—I will not vouch for you. Though, no one has been caught before.*"

"Mucho gusto," Marco said.

"I will check on you, sometimes."

Marco stepped into the crate, but Sheila would not follow. The captain's footsteps gradually faded farther away. When they could no longer be heard, Marco said "Get in here."

Sheila took a step back. "No way. If—God forbid—we were to run into something, we would sink to the bottom of the ocean in that thing."

"We could obviously leave the box then. It's just a precaution. Come on, they're doing us a *huge* favor. The least we can do is to abide by their rules."

Sheila's chest rose as she took a giant breath through her nose. Finally, she joined him in the solid case. Marco lifted the door handle and pulled the door closed with a strong effort. The door latched shut with a boom.

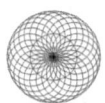

Chapter 18

BLACKNESS SHALL
CONSUME

Portis sat in the navigational bridge holding his head in his hands. The bridge was empty, all the officers relieved of their current duty.

Not only had the crowd on the deck grown exponentially, but they were completely out of control. The police had been forced away, and Mary had gone missing. Order was almost non-existent.

He had set out to locate Mary, scanning the entire deck to no avail. The casinos and shopping mall were nearly empty, and of the people he did pass, none of them paid any resemblance to the beautiful purser. He pictured her in some utility hall, overwhelmed and crying from the unheeded stress. It strung at his conscious because he knew it was partially his fault for delegating full passenger responsibility to her. At first, he thought it was in her realm of responsibility, but upon experiencing firsthand the ruthlessness of the passengers, Portis knew he had made a mistake.

He should have stepped up to the plate at the start, when the machine had come into view and so many questions had erupted out of thin air. It would have made for a more acceptable explanation coming from the captain, for people base knowledge upon such things as titles and positions. Portis knew that just because a man was a king, it didn't make him altogether powerful, just as a school teacher was not infinitely knowledgeable. The only thing titles do are to specify duties, not to clarify a person's capabilities.

Biases also would have led to believe that a beautiful *woman* would not be able to deal with the situation. It was an ignorance that had not put Mary out of commission, but probably had hurt her feelings a great deal. Portis knew that one prejudice was true—women were more sensitive.

Pete was off securing the life boats, incognito. The Quartermaster was certain they should be deployed, but Portis wasn't on the same page. The passengers were unaware of the disaster below the upper deck, and once it was discovered, there would be mayhem. There would be cause to vacate the boat once that happened, but until then, Portis found no reason to worry the passengers any further. He also knew that if action didn't take place at the perfect moment, there would be mutiny.

It was only a matter of time, quickly diminishing time, before all hell broke loose. Portis was terrified. As much as he tried to have a tough exterior, his interior was not to match. His ex-girlfriend had called him King-Tough-the-Cream-Puff, referring to his lack of confidence in his own action and inability to stand up for himself.

For some reason, though, something about the impending doom made him re-evaluate his decisiveness. It's why he stood against the man on deck. He knew that if he wanted to live, then quick thinking and important choices were first priority. Oh, and if he ever wanted to snag Mary, once it all blew over.

The boat rocked with enough force to jar all of the items off of his bookshelf. The nautical clock his brother had given him smashed into hundreds of tiny pieces. Portis grabbed onto the counter and the edge of the controls for dear life. They were slowly drifting away from the machine, its speed had steadied and the waves came non-frequently. It was taking a long time, but Portis hoped that eventually they would float far enough away that the engines would work once more.

He tried to fire them up, but the button only clicked, a dead initiator on an otherwise dead vessel. Portis sighed and picked up the VHF radio.

"Mayday, mayday, mayday. Splendid, Splendid, Splendid. Captain Portis calling all ships... we have complete engine failure. Repeat, complete engine failure. If you can hear me..."

He waited a beat, for he thought there was a fizzle on the other end. No answer ever came. Portis looked out the window, past the giant waves and spinning spire, for a sign of any ship, any plane, but only saw far spread water.

He tried again. "Mayday, mayday, mayday." Still no answer.

Before, he must not have noticed that on the surface of the ocean, bobbing like fishing lures, were thousands of dead fish. In his fascination with the machine, he had forgotten about anything beyond the ship. Yet, he was amazed that he could have possibly missed them. The dead fish, sharks, jellyfish, covered nearly the entire surface surrounding the machine. It looked to Portis as if a large grey piece of construction paper had been glued on top of the ocean and sprinkled with silver glitter.

The sight worried Portis, for how many fish had perished? Had more machines popped up in other places? If so, then what—if anything—remained living?

He knew the planet survived as does any living body, by exactly balanced equilibrium. When your fingers wrinkle, it's because they have a higher salt concentration than the water, so the liquid is absorbed and bloats your cells. Just as he knew if all the creatures in the sea perished, seventy percent of Earth's oxygen would cease to form. It was just another reason that things such as oil spills and pollution are detrimental to the environment. Easily said, if the creatures in the ocean died, so would the human race.

In order to self-preserve, humans needed to look past themselves, past their insignificance, and realize that we are but one contribution to the millions of species which create an ecosystem unlike any other in the known universe. Portis stared at the dead creatures atop the endless blue and decided there must be something else at work.

Chapter 19

A FRIEND

O f late, Sal had been getting excruciating headaches. They would come out of nowhere and stab through his skull. He attributed them to the machines, but wasn't sure if it was really the case. He hoped they were to blame, for he wasn't sure if the hospitals were in any working order. No sirens had passed by in a long while. Either nobody had been hurt nearby or—more likely—the emergency drivers had given up. Things were starting to escalate.

The temperature had dropped to below forty by the gauge of his indoor thermometer. Soon enough it would be snowing in Southern California, he thought.

In keeping with the chill, Sal opened the freezer and extracted a frozen Swanson's dinner. He threw the thing in the microwave, plastic wrap and all, and hit the number five button on the microwave pad. It whirred alive, the light inside activating. He watched the processed shit go round-and-round, bent over and desperate for nutrition that wasn't truly there, until one of the piercing headaches attacked him.

Sal staggered away from the microwave, his feet dragging helplessly as he tripped toward the front door. For some unexplainable reason, he wanted to see the sun, feel the warmth on his skin. His brain felt tight in the casing of his skull.

The glint of the sun—shrouded by miles of foggy colored clouds— touched his skin, but offered no solace. He closed his eyes and fell forward face first, as he dug in his pockets for the keys to his Porsche.

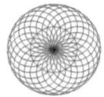

When Sal came around, two bespectacled, beady eyes stared into his drowsy face. They were Norman Blanchett's.

"Quite a spill," his neighbor said.

Sal sat up in an enamored fashion. His wrist hurt from landing on top of it at a crooked angle. He had blacked out when he fell, for how long he knew not. It was good to hear the voice of another *live* human, despite the fact that it was Mr. Nosy's. After thinking about it, he realized that not only had he never talked to the man, but he'd never actually heard the man's silky voice, never expected it to sound so *sweet*. In his mind, Sal had always heard a curmudgeonly old bastard.

"Hurts like hell," Sal said. "How long was I down for the count?"

Norman smiled. "Only a few seconds... thirty at most." He rustled his hands inside of his windbreaker and revealed a small plastic bag wrapped in a paper towel.

"I brought you an ice pack. I've been keeping 'em handy. Thought you might need it. Do you feel all right?"

"Nauseous... my brain feels like something is swimming around inside."

Norman offered Sal his hand. He gripped it reluctantly, bestowing a gift of a sweaty palm upon his neighbor. On his feet, Sal felt dizzy.

"Must be having the headaches. I've been getting them on and off, too. Never that bad, though. They peak especially when you're near electrical equipment. It's as if they're conducting, or transmitting."

Sal thought on it. He had been bending over looking into the door of the microwave, something his mother had always warned him not to do. Maybe the machines were intensifying the microwaves.

"I was using the microwave."

Norman nodded, satisfied. "What for?"

"Tv dinner... minus the tv."

Norman chuckled. "Come on over to my place. I've got steak and potatoes ready."

Sal imagined steak and potatoes. Grocery stores had been out of the stuff for weeks. He looked into the old man's face, warm and welcoming. Perhaps, he thought, the old man was more interesting than he had once thought—mysterious, but interesting.

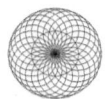

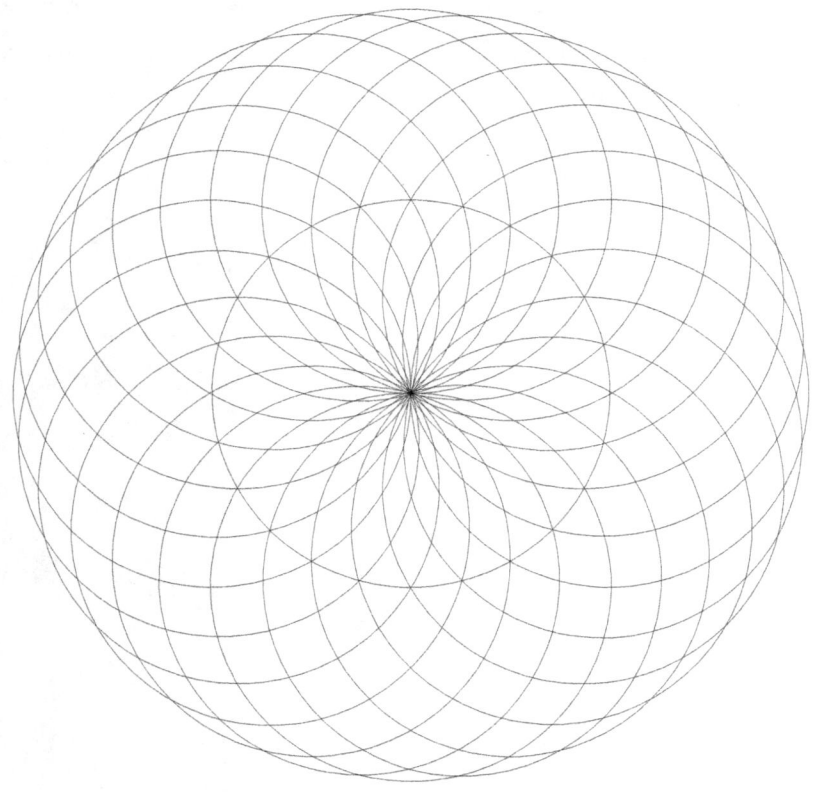

Chapter 20

FAMILIAR HORIZONS

In the corner of the crate was a table that Marco had not seen on first inspection of the room. A checkerboard was laid into the tabletop. They had played innumerable games, until Sheila became bored. It was also difficult to remember where your chips were with them sliding around.

Sheila sat on the very edge of the cot with her head down. Her elbows rested on her knees and her hair hung over her face. Marco sat in a chair with his foot on the edge of the table, leaning backwards on two of the chair's legs. He flipped a red checker and caught it, repeatedly.

"How long until we're there, do you think?" he asked her.

Sheila gingerly raised her head and let out a long yawn. Crow's feet formed at the corners of her eyes, making her look older than her years. "Days and days and days."

She yawned once more.

Marco sat forward and placed the checker back on the table. The checkers were evenly spaced, strategically. He thought of the machines and how somebody must have built them. Why and when, he wondered. Were they also placed strategically? He stared at them for a long time, then realizing he was spacing out, opened his eyes wide.

Sheila was also staring off, seeming to look through the door of the crate.

"What are you thinking about, babe?"

Sheila turned toward Marco solemnly. "Whether or not we should stop and see my parents."

Being close to his mother, Marco couldn't understand the argument proving contest. He *needed* to see his mother. He thought about her often, sent thoughts into the atmosphere, praying that she was physically and mentally stable. She had very few friends in America, mainly her knitting club.

Sheila's parents were divorced and both remarried, living in the same region of New York State. It would be an easy-enough stop, if she cared. What she really needed to do was to search inside and realize that she loved her parents, despite how sour she was toward them sometimes, especially over the divorce.

Marco stood and walked to the cot. He sat and wrapped his arm over her shoulder. "We can stop there if you like. It's not a problem."

He pecked her on the cheek. "I actually think we should."

She looked him deep in the eyes. "Are you sure you're okay with it?"

"Of course, you know I don't say things I don't mean."

"I mean… I'm still not entirely sure I want to. What if…?"

They lay down side by side, Marco gently easing her to resting position, until his knees were in the back of hers. "Things will be just fine."

Minutes later they were fast asleep on the gently rocking cargo ship, proceeding through dangerous waters.

Marco awoke from a loud bang on the door. His eyes flapped open. He shook Sheila a little bit. "Hey! *Wake up!*"

She startled awake. "What? What?" She was obviously on edge.

"Somebody knocked."

"What time is it?"

Marco let out a held-back laugh. "Does it really make a difference anymore?"

He cracked the heavy door and peeked through the crack. There was a fair amount of light peeking through the space, much brighter than the light inside of the crate. The captain lay in wait beyond the threshold, his thick knuckles ready to rap on the steel door once more.

"*Thought you may be hungry. Here, enjoy.*" He nodded and walked off, after pushing a small cart on wheels toward the opening. Two stainless steel warmers sat atop the cart. A thin plane of steam escaped from the sides of both, bouncing off the two tall glasses filled with water. Perspiration leaked off the sides.

Marco lifted the cart over the doorframe jutting from the floor, and rolled it into their makeshift bedroom. "Dinner is served, madam."

Sheila sat up, pulled her hair back, and crossed one leg on the bed. "Good, I'm starving."

He unveiled the meals. Two fish looking fresh out of the water stared deadly back. There were also piles of greenery which looked like seaweed or kelp.

Marco said, "When in Rome..." and started to slice the aquatic feast.

Sheila poked at the meat, acted as if she couldn't cut through the shiny skin. "I hate when they still have their head. Looks like something off of a Chinese menu."

She lifted a forkful of the green leaves to her face, and then quickly pulled it away. "Ugh... smells awful."

Marco tasted the fish. It wasn't terrible. Dry and salted, but nothing worse than you'd receive at a typical seaside restaurant. He was the type to stand anything edible, try any new foods. He figured it was the way he was raised, essentially as a Spaniard. Americans, like Sheila, are much more closed minded concerning variety in meals.

Sheila dropped her fork on the plate. "I wish I had a *big* juicy steak right now."

She mimicked eating the flank of a cow, taking a larger than necessary bite. "And some onion rings… mmmmm."

He had to admit—it sounded delicious. Looking at the bland meal on his plate, his stomach rumbled. It would fill him up, but probably not satiate his hunger. Knowing it would be the sort of food delegated for his consumption (or worse) in the coming months, all Marco could do was to fork the tads of over-salted fish into his mouth, dreaming of that fat piece of Angus.

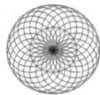

Chapter 21

SHIPS ASSAIL

The rain was falling hard on the deck of the ship, collecting on benches and finally forcing passengers inside. This had become a cause for concern for Portis. Not only were the passengers inside, but it was time to set sail. He knew that the people would be gathering and discovering the locked stairwells. Surely some of them would have family or belongings below deck, and would realize that something terrible must have happened.

Portis sent Pete, Mary, and the two police to rally the passengers to the foyer of the shopping mall—to again do his bidding. Once there, Portis would announce the fate of the dead and ultimately that they would have to endeavor over the wide blue.

He feared the move to the lifeboats, for the waves peaked sometimes at fifteen feet above sea level, if not higher. The climate was tense, the sky deep blue with highlights of black-grey storm clouds. Streaks of fluorescent yellow shot through the atmosphere. Yet, he knew the worst was to come. The climate aboard the ship would rival the weather, and some. He was going to be forced into explanations that he didn't possess.

Why did he allow the below deck passengers to remain there? Why didn't they turn around when the radar had been up and running? Why hadn't they deployed the lifeboats before the storm had begun?

They were all understandable questions—ones which Portis had already played over and over in his mind. The answers just weren't as readily available as the wavering inquisitions.

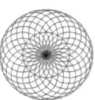

The halls were nearly empty. Pete imagined the voyagers were inside their rooms. He knocked on a door, room 314. After trying once more, he withdrew Portis's universal key, which unlocked all doors aboard the ship. He walked inside. Clothes were scattered everywhere, belongings dropped on the coffee table, and the trash full to bursting. No humans.

A woman opened the next door a crack. She had a pretty face, covered in freckles. Two blonde boys bounced across the room behind her, they couldn't have been older than five or six. The woman's green eyes acknowledged Pete's badge and she smiled.

"Can I help you?"

He wasn't sure how she could be smiling under such dire circumstances. Then, some people just have that natural optimism. Pete wasn't sure if it was his years in the military or unstable adolescence, but he tended toward the dark and narcissistic, always plotting for the worst-case scenario.

"Ma'am, we're evacuating to the shopping mall. Our Captain has an announcement."

Her smile faded into a look of deep concern. Pete figured it had something to do with her two beautiful, red-faced boys. She covered her mouth with the bottom of her palm.

"Oh, dear… is everything okay?" Her brow furrowed and bottom lip sucked under her top lip.

"Everything is under control."

Even as he said it, Pete didn't believe his own statement, and was sure that he didn't sound very convincing. Their future was uncertain.

She thanked him and closed the door. Pete stood there for a moment, rubbing the back of his neck. Through the door he could hear the muffled voice of the woman asking the children if they wanted to go to the mall. The boys dually protested, wanting to stay home and play.

Pete turned his attention toward the corridor. The next door was another non-answer. As he turned the corner, the emergency speakers cut off the overhead instrumental music, some soothing jazz.

"Attention… this is your Captain speaking. I request that all passengers report to the starboard side shopping plaza. We are clearly in a state of emergency. Therefore, I have a very important announcement. Remain calm, we have everything under control. Again, please report to the shopping center off of starboard side. Thank you."

Way to word it, thought Pete. *We are clearly in a state of emergency.* If the passengers didn't have a reason to worry before, they did now. The easiest way to cause widespread panic is to inform the people that everything is under control. Yet, that was the verbiage Portis wanted him to use. It leads them to distrust you—if everything was under control nobody would need to reassure to the fact.

When Pete walked around the next corner, he stumbled upon a man fidgeting with one of the doors to the lower decks. He was bent over and trying to shove something into the lock, obviously trying to breach it.

"Can I help you?" Pete asked.

The man stood fast. He was balding with a horseshoe around his ears, of black hair. "Damn door is stuck or something. I was trying to get down to my room."

Pete straightened his spine, standing tall to let the man know he had the power. "Sir, the lower decks are currently locked off. There was an accident down there."

The man dropped the coat hanger from his hand. "What kind of accident? What in God's name do you mean?"

"Just come down to the shopping mall and we'll explain—"

"To hell with that!" the man said, spitting onto Pete's arm. "My wife is down there."

Pete swallowed hard. He hoped the man didn't catch the small action. In the military he'd learned to read body language and knew that swallowing implied nervousness. His composure was faltering.

The passenger took a step closer, coming within reach. "Open the door, *buddy*."

"Sir, I'm—"

He shoved Pete in the chest with his two large mitts. "I said open that *fucking* door."

Pete wondered what made the man think he even had the power to do so. Unless, had he seen him with the captain? As usual, however, the man had mistakenly pushed Pete, underestimated him. Where others had restraint, he did not.

"I understand that you're upset… but I'll tell you only once. Touch me again and you're on the ground."

The man gritted his teeth in anger and lunged forward. It was like slow motion. Pete could swear he'd seen the black hairs in high definition, covering the passing arm, as he grabbed above the elbow and piled a knee into his spine. The man crumpled to one knee, with Pete holding his thick wrist behind his back and pushing it toward his head in a chicken wing.

"I warned you, man." He blew out a deep breath. The man started to struggle, but Pete yanked his arm higher. He grunted into submission and fell forward, placing his other hand on the floor.

"I don't want to hurt you, man—but I will. We're meeting at the mall, you can come or not. I really don't give two shits. One way or another I have to do my job. And I don't have a *damn* thing to lose, but my life."

"Okay, okay…" the guy huffed through a blockage of pain.

Pete pushed his arm forward and the man caught himself on all fours. "Just tell me what happened."

"I couldn't tell ya'. All I know is that everyone below deck is dead." He thought it would have been harder to say, harder to explain. Maybe he had become hardened beyond a point of emotion from all those years of informing military wives of their husbands' deaths.

The bald man clutched at Pete's legs, disbelief filling his eyes. "It's not true! You're just kidding. Say it's not true!"

His eyes filled and as he started to sob, he tucked his face into Pete's leg. He could feel the man's tears wetting his thigh, but didn't mind. It was the most he could do after delivering the worst news of the man's life.

As the man sat there, racking, Pete thought of his own life. How many people did he have that were close enough to cry over? His parents were dead and he never married, never had any siblings or birthed any children. He could think of only one man for whom he would do anything, for whom he would spend his life; a man he highly admired.

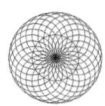

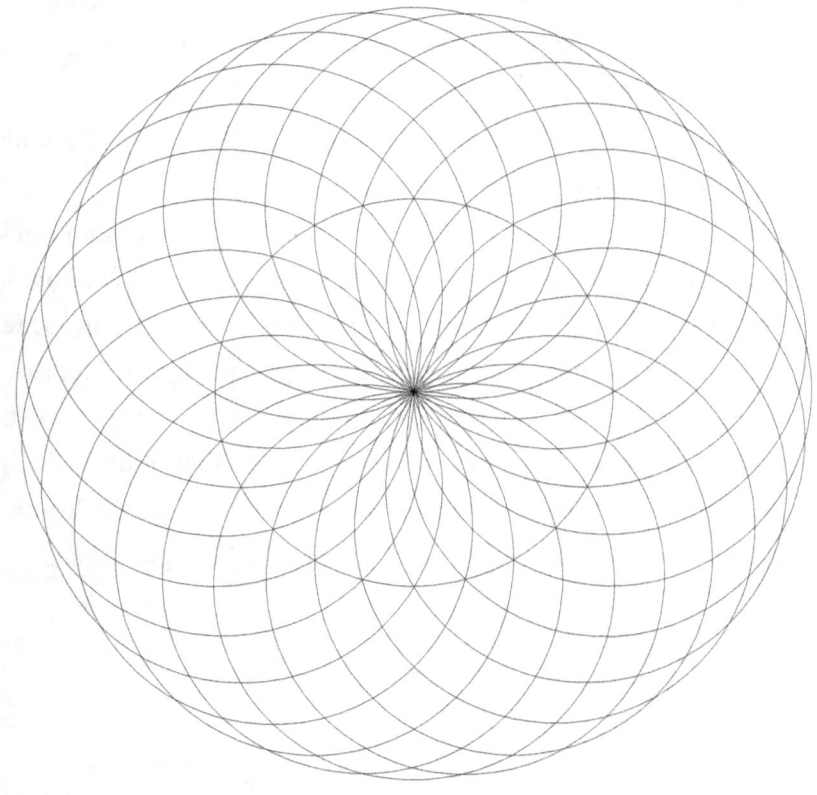

Chapter 22

NEW WORLD

"It's only a matter of time before the electricity is off, too," Norman told Sal.

He sliced the fat steak in front of him, placed a triangle in his mouth, and chewed it to bits. "You see…" He swallowed.

"Soon enough, the oil companies gonna jack their prices so high that there'll be nobody who wants to buy. We're talking two, three hundred a barrel. Never mind when the workers stop showing up."

"People will start syphoning gas, then."

Norman blew out air. "Hell, people will start killing each other for bread soon enough. Ya' never realize our dependencies. Everything's brought in from places out East. Nothing's local anymore. Without that oil, we ain't getting nothing."

Sal used the side of his fork to scrape up the last of the *real* potatoes on his plate. He savored them to the final spud. For Norman was right, once oil supplies started to dwindle, the country would go into disrepair. He would be scrounging just for his frozen dinners.

"Where'd you get all this good food? Last time I went to the store they barely had any produce, let alone meats."

Norman smiled and pushed another forkful of mashed potatoes into mouth. He took a big drink of milk. "Let's just say I know people who know people."

He pointed his fork at Sal, then. The way he did it bothered Sal, as if he was pointedly saying to watch your step, or even to be on his good graces. Sal didn't know what Norman was capable of—the man was such an enigma. One minute he was spying on Sal, the next he's inviting him over for dinner.

He decided to push the envelope. "And these people…how long can they keep you well fed?"

Norman smiled again and placed his fork on the round table. "Oh, years and years. Their supplies are many."

Sal blinked twice. His vision was a bit blurry, as if dust had covered his eyes. With his thumb and forefinger, he rubbed at his closed eyes and then opened his mouth. His jaw felt tight, hard to open. When he lifted his eyelids, his vision was worse. "I can't see anything," he told Norman.

From across the table a few light-hearted chuckles drifted. "You don't think I know that? None of us see anything. Until it's too late, that is."

Sal went to stand, but his legs gave up and he fell back in his seat, almost toppling over. "What's happeren?" He couldn't speak straight. It was hard to swallow, mouth dry and sticky.

"You didn't think I get my supplies for free, did you? We gotta work for our till in this country."

Through the haze covering his eyeballs, Sal could see the old man stand and start to circulate the table. Sal fell forward onto the table. Norman's hand caressed the back of his neck until he was unconscious.

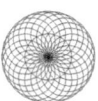

He could hear the thrum of an engine—sand crushing underneath tires—as he bopped around limply. Sal opened his eyes to witness blackness.

He was in a vehicle carrying over rough terrain—that much he could tell. He tried to sit up, but his wrists were handcuffed or bound somehow.

"Hey!" he yelled. "You fucking *drugged* me? I'm going to kill you, Norman. You *hear* me? You're fucked buddy! Just wait. Wait until I'm free and you're fucking *dead*!"

It took all of Sal's effort, but he was able to roll onto his back. His head was swimming, spinning, and his vision still blurred, and obscured by a piece of almost see through black felt. "Where in the hell are you taking me?"

He could hear the sound of someone shifting on leather, like a giant fart. Over the top of the seat there appeared the shadow of a head, shoulder, and an arm. The arm started to drop down. Sal tried to turn away, but before he could react, something metal connected with the bridge of his nose. He felt a hard crack and blood poured out into his screaming mouth.

"Shut the *fuck* up!" a hearty voice commanded.

Sal spit the blood onto his shirt, but it continued flowing. "Am I going to die?"

The man, who sounded like an African-American, said, "We're all going to die." The metal smashed into Sal's broken nose again, sending white spots of light to the back of his eyelids and searing pain into the middle of his face.

He could feel his face was indented, while he rolled from side to side. It felt like a giant brick was on his face, and bees were stinging his cheeks all over. He didn't speak again, instead, trying his best not to cry. The pain was like nothing he'd ever felt before, and he couldn't help but groan.

He'd made a mistake in trusting Norman. It was all too good to be true—free dinner, unlimited grocery. Nothing came without a price. He should've known.

Taking things for granted always worked against you. Like thinking that after the world went to hell, people would automatically start to care for each other. Like assuming maybe he could let his guard down and have a relationship with a person again, even just as a friend. Lying in the backseat of the bumpy vehicle, Sal regressed and realized he'd been right before. The only person in the world he could trust was the big number one.

The car rolled to a stop and two car doors slammed. Above his head, another creaked open on rusty hinges. Two meaty hands grabbed his shoulders and yanked him into the sand. He was pushed through the sand, until he rolled onto his back. Whoever was holding him captive had blindfolded him.

Sal was yanked to his feet and forced to walk ahead of his captors with his head hung low. He had never felt the barrel of a gun, but considered that whatever was pressing into his back was fairly close to how it should feel. Everything was like a bad scene in a movie. He was drugged and driven into the desert. Next, he would probably be killed. He felt like he was in *Casino*.

They stopped for a moment and the blindfold was torn off his head. The gate ahead of them was protecting a small complex made of concrete. Men in army garb stood sentinel with automatic rifles slung over their shoulders. As they passed through the opening in the gate, one of the guards—whose face was blocked by the visor on his helmet—said "Hey, Chuck."

Sal had an inkling that neither of his kidnappers was actually named Chuck—that it served as a guise. He wondered how a fake name would protect the man. Oh, he would tell the authorities: One of their names was "Chuck". Even if they used solely first names, it wouldn't make a difference. There would be absolutely no way to track that.

"Chuck," who happened to be the African-American, said "How's it going?"

It implied that maybe Chuck had not been to the complex in some time, that he had been off elsewhere, maybe watching somebody. Could they have been watching him for an extended period? He shuddered to think that more than Norman's eyes had been trained on him, for who knows how long.

Beyond the first gate was yet another fence, with barbed wire wrapped around the top perimeter. Sal's vision had returned enough so that he could read the bright orange sign on the chain. It read, "Caution: High Voltage."

They stopped at the fence, there was a loud buzz, and a partition of the chain slid out of the way to allow them passage. Sal was again shoved forward, their sacrifice, their collateral.

The building ahead was low to the ground and square. The roof was flat and coated with black gravel. Sal tried to obey and walk farther forward, but was pulled in reverse by the handcuffs. One of the captors passed him, withdrew a card from his pocket, and pushed it into the wall of the building like an ATM machine. There was another buzz and a door opened into the complex.

Finally, Sal was granted a complete view of one of their faces. He was a white guy with thick eyebrows, high cheekbones, and loaded with pock marks—your typical Metallica-loving white trash. "Get inside," he said.

A stairwell ventured into uninterrupted blackness with Sal guiding the pack. He couldn't see the steps below and relied on his inherent directional abilities to carry him onward. When finally at the bottom (he could tell because of the door blocking his way), he was again yanked backwards and nearly slipped on the damp stamps.

The white guy said, "Steer clear." He shoved Sal with his shoulder and took the card out, which had opened the previous door. It slid away, disappearing into the wall like the first had, and the Caucasian captor entered. The track in the floor told Sal that the small room was an elevator. What scared him was that there was only one direction for it to travel, unless it ventured sideways and diagonally like Wonka's.

Above them the air was being sucked through a vent. Sal could feel that the air was thinner inside of the space. Then again, he could have been hyperventilating. The elevator came to a smooth stop and the door rolled open with a gasp. What Sal beheld was nothing short of spectacular.

They stood on a balcony, overlooking a compound filled with greens. Rows upon rows of vegetables grew between wide walls, surrounded by giant metal pillars. Men in t-shirts picked from the plants, placing their gather into baskets. Extremely bright white lights, nearly blinding, shone down from the ceiling. The field seemed to stretch for miles, until stopping at a wall of glass. Behind the panes was a white room containing men in Hazmat suits. They bustled about, handling different items and running machines, working.

Sal was moved to the left, toward another stairwell, which descended into the farming compound. Through the dried blood at the base of his nostrils, he smelt manure. It was actually a pleasing scent, reminiscent of back road country drives his parents had taken him on in New England as a boy.

"Welcome to Chamber One," the man holding his arms said.

Chamber One meant that there were more to be seen. Sal looked at the high ceiling and examined the pillars. How long had it taken to build the underground facility? Had the country been planning on something of this magnitude, some sort of worldwide disaster?

A set of keys jangled behind Sal's back and the restraint on his right wrist relieved, and then his left. The black man said, "Welcome to the world as you now know it."

Chapter 23

SO LONG...

"Let's settle down, let's settle down," Portis commanded.

The crowd was unruly, would not relax by any means. People continued to flock into the large entry hall of the shopping center, filling it to the brink of explosion, almost like a rock concert. Mary was continually focused on circulating and trying to quiet the people so that Portis would have a window of speaking opportunity. Her hair was a flutter of fire, spreading through the ocean of humans.

He could hear her voice loud and frustrated over the cacophony. "*Listen up*! The Captain has an important announcement."

He tried to speak, himself, but felt he was not given but a shred of attention. None of the faces concerned themselves with him, just continued to converse with one another on erroneous matters.

"Excuse me, everyone... *Excuse me*!" He raised his hand into the air. With his other hand he put two fingers in his mouth and let out a sharp whistle. "*Hey*! Listen up. You've all been very curious about what is going to happen. I'm going to be frank... the engines will not turn back on. Hundreds are dead beneath this deck."

There was a collective gasp. People shifted around the room, looking for those they knew, whispering in worried tones.

"Basically, we've decided it in the passengers' best interest to deploy the life boats. We will start..."

The room exploded with shouts and people tried to shift to the front of the mass, trying to talk to Portis. He stood strong on his soap box, which was really a metal chair. "I understand your concern—"

"You don't understand," a woman yelled. "I've got children on this boat."

Portis had to laugh. He obviously had no idea how precious children were until this angry mom told him. "As I said, I understand your concern. However, if we stay here on this cruise ship, we will eventually run out of food. We'll need to start rationing—"

"And who's coming to save us on those wee boats?" asked a non-American accent. "I haven't seen any planes or boats pass by. How about when our food runs out on those toys?"

There was a gathering of agreement on the air, people joining together again. Portis was trying to be the voice of reason, but when your own confidence is wavering, how can one convince others to jump ship?

"Look, let's work together and—"

"Screw that," said the Brit. "I ain't going out on those tiny rafts. I'm staying here on this humongous boat." The older man with cropped hair shook his head in defiance. There would be no amount of words that could swap his decision. Even with force it would be a wasteful battle.

Portis made a bold decision. "Whoever wants to remain aboard is welcome to do so. I am nobody's keeper, especially in this time."

He jumped off of his chair and made his way through the crowd. Whoever wanted to follow him was more than welcome to do so, but as far as he was concerned, it had turned into every man for himself. On his way, he passed the Brit wearing a snobbish grin below a thick mustache.

"So much for going down with the ship, eh?"

Portis chewed on his cheek, trying not to react, while inside he was bursting. Despite losing his cool during the announcement—and completely giving up—he still had a very small hint of composure.

He'd always been in control, but now it felt like the reigns had been let go. He had handed them over to Lady Fate, to do with them what she will. People moved out of the way for him as if he were a sick disease. Portis wondered who they thought would lend them to safety, if not him. The Brit? The douche in the Polo?

He could tell they were loose cannons, relying on his answers for some small comfort. What was he a preacher? The only thing he could be sure of was that the machine spinning was nothing Godly, and being close to it was only going to make matters worse.

Pete had started to double check the life boats—to verify that there were no holes and that each had enough lifejackets. No way was he deploying them unless they were completely safe.

Behind one of the boats was propped an empty bottle of booze. It clunked onto the deck as he shifted the boat way from the davits. He lifted the bottle upside-down and a spare amount of liquor ran out onto his jeans. "Damn it."

Pete was about to chuck the bottle overboard, but realized that he hadn't truly given the machine much thought. He had been assessing the immediate danger—the engines not working and being stuck on a boat—but hadn't really associated the cause. Being a man of reason, it was against his usual behavior to deny the thoughts. Yet, he had. It stood to reason that there must have been a purpose for the machines surfacing when they did. Something like that doesn't just happen.

In the army you shoot because you were shot at, provoked. What had provoked the machines that were causing unusual weather, seemingly dropping temperatures and thinning the air? He looked down at the bottle in his hand, out to the wide ocean—deep, dark blue, and innocent—and wondered. Was it man's fault?

Portis walked next to Mary. He could see her hand swinging at her side and wanted to grab it. Behind them walked employees of the shopping mall, the casino, the restaurants, more deck officers, and then the passengers. He could see Pete ahead, lifting the boats into the air with the help of the bowling alley employees, readying them for descent and departure.

He waved to Pete, who gave a quick nod and then went back to work. The boat rocked starboard and Portis steadied into a defensive stance. Behind him followed gasps and terror.

"Holy shit!" Mary quipped.

He looked at her shocked face. Never before had he felt such a quake, and understood her surprise at the near capsizing of the vessel. A wave racked the side of the ship and Portis stumbled, but remained upright. He turned to see an elderly woman fall into the side of one of the uprights.

A man—whom Portis assumed was her husband—groped for her, but failed. "Jeanne!" he yelled.

The woman hit with an un-cushioned slam and Portis could only assume something had been broken, considering her age. Much to his surprise, the woman stood, not without a look of pain etched onto her face. The waves momentarily abated and Portis waved everyone forward again. "Come on, folks."

The sea was at turmoil and though it was dangerous to take to the open waters, Portis had a feeling that it would not be much longer before the ship would be swallowed whole by Poseidon. He started to usher passengers onto the life boats, not separating families. They had plenty of vessels to spare.

"Take a group and fill the next boat," he told Mary. "Twenty per device."

"Okay. Should I get on as well?"

He could see her throat move with a swallow. "I'm scared. What if we run out of food and water?"

"Pete loaded the ships, plus we have the extra bags." He indicated the emergency bag slung over his shoulder. "We have a better chance of locating another ship, or an island, rather than staying aboard."

"I hope you're right." She turned to the passengers. "There's a lot of life left to be lived."

Portis's eyes wandered through the crowd, accounting the passengers' ages, examining expressions. They ranged from babies to the elderly, unaffected to the alarmed. Without a true count, Portis attempted a rough estimate of how many heads had followed. Give or take, one hundred and fifty, he guessed—also, a lot of life to lose.

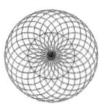

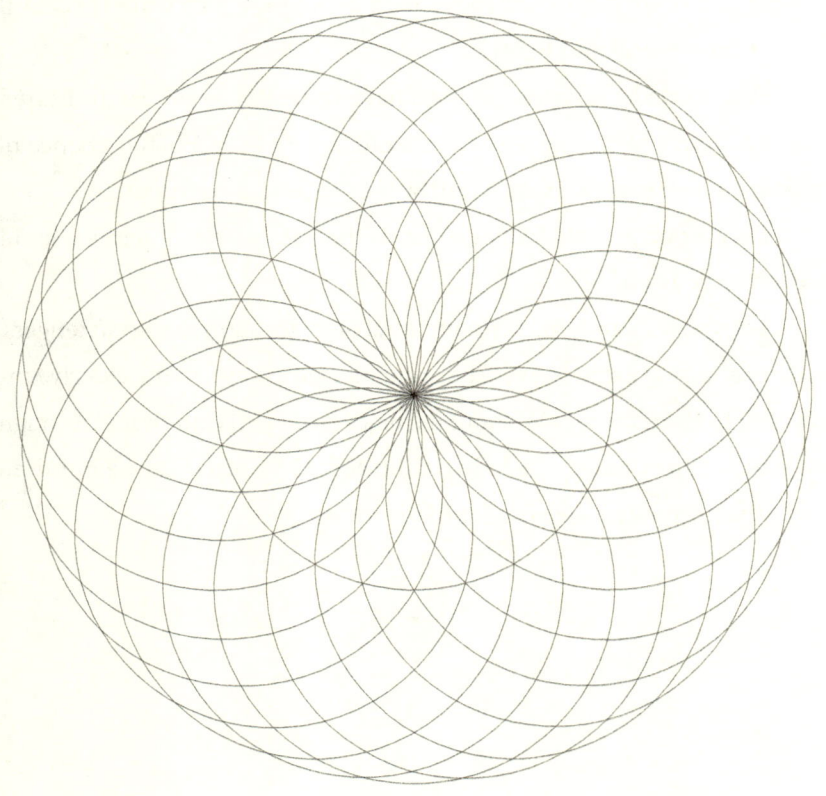

Chapter 24

ON THE BOATS AND
ON THE PLANES

The rocking of the ship had become almost sickening, certainly hypnotic. Marco lay on his side, one hand holding his stomach, the other over his eyes. He felt like he was on the amusement park ride where the wooden ship swings on long poles. He wanted a bucket nearby, just in case of an emergency. Sheila was tucked into his body, rubbing his back gently.

"Feeling any better?" she asked.

"No. I feel like I'm going to hurl."

"I'm sorry, babe. Take some deep breaths."

When he was ill, she really understood how to soothe him. She cupped and rubbed his head. He felt like a pampered child with his mother looking after him. It made him realize how much simpler it is when you're young and ignorant to the ways of the world. You can live without worry, with others looking after you.

The floating hulk lurched downward, dropping a surprising amount, and making Marco's guts squeeze. He couldn't hold it. He jumped to his feet, making the rusty springs under the cot screech.

"Don't go out—," Sheila started to say to him, but the immediacy in his stomach blocked her out. He was out of the crate and bolting for the bathroom. They typically waited for either the captain or another shipmate to come around (usually once an hour) to go to the bathroom, but this was an exception. He had to get there.

A forklift drove past the hall ahead of him. Marco turned right down the perpendicular passage. His mouth was full of air. He was trying to push the puke back down. He slammed through the metal door, into the six-foot-wide toilet. He aimed for the stains ringing the bowl and let it go just in time.

His ribs squeezed tight, constricting on his organs. Pressure pushed outward on his skull, as he expelled his insides. He kneeled on one knee, panting.

When the captain said, "*Motion sickness?*" he nearly shit himself.

Marco nodded without turning.

"*You all done?*"

The words reminded him of the fire in his throat and Marco let go another round of chunks. He closed his eyes in pain. With his head tilted down and his hand on the back of the toilet, he said "*I think that's it.*"

"*Good. Get back to the room*, porfavor."

Marco stood weakly. Throwing up always drained him. "*Do you have the time?*"

"*Nine o'clock.*"

"*At night?*"

"*Yes, can you not tell?*"

Marco wiped the vomit from his nose and then washed his hands. "No..." he said over the running sink. "*Don't you know we're in the dark?*"

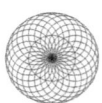

The ship docked the sixth morning, almost perfectly as assumed. A bang came on the door of the crate. Marco had heard it so often that he knew the bosses plea.

"All set," he said. "*Port Authority security has already inspected and cleared the ship.*"

"*Now what happens?*"

"*You'll have to stay inside for now. You'll be lifted by a forklift and placed into a tractor trailer. There's one more thing you'll need to do… lie under the cot.*"

"*Why is that?*"

"*Customs will also scan each load with radiation.*"

"*So, we're going to get caught, then.*" Marco's heart started to beat faster. He knew things could not possibly go seamlessly.

The captain raised his hand. "*No, no. We have an agreement with our scanner. He never scans under the bed. I told you… we've not been caught before. It's a science.*"

"*Wouldn't a bed be suspicious anyway? It would imply someone living inside.*"

"*Can't report what you don't see. Just stay underneath the cot and everything will be fine.*"

After the captain bid farewell, Marco revealed the unfortunate news to Sheila. He felt sorry for having brought her. Here he was putting her at risk, but if it came down to it, he would offer himself as collateral for her freedom.

They lay under the bed on their stomachs. Marco tried to wrap his arm around her numerous times, but she only pushed him away.

"Please, I'm sorry…" he said, trying to hold her.

"Just don't *touch* me." She was crying and he hated it when she cried, especially when it was his fault she was upset.

"Everything's going to be all right," Marco said. "Captain Rafael said they've dealt with this a million times. He's got people in his pocket."

"Oh, so I should feel better that you placed me in the hands of organized criminals?"

"They're not…" He wanted to say they weren't criminals because they were doing something righteous, but they *were* breaking federal laws.

"If I thought we were going to get caught, you know I never would have asked you to come."

Sheila sniffed. "You would've come without me, you said."

Marco could tell she had been holding on to something, holding a grudge, from the way she had been distant to the small frowns she'd been making the entire ride.

"I'm sorry. I'll never leave you again."

She looked him in the eyes. "Promise?"

"Yes. You're my one true love."

She locked lips with him, lying there under the bed. To Marco it had started to feel like the end of the world, but tasting Sheila's breath—the scent it possessed—her salty tears, brought him to a different planet, made him feel like there would never be an end.

Eventually she stopped crying and he just held her. The crate lifted into the air on wobbly supports and started to move. He prayed that their temporary home would be granted clearance. When the crate was dropped with a gentle thud, Marco could breathe.

Sheila whispered, "What now?"

"I guess we wait and be quiet."

"For what? Are we going on foot?"

"By truck. I don't know where they're taking us, but wherever it is I'll take care of you."

"Thank you, baby."

The movement of the truck was much smoother and they carried on for hours. Marco and Sheila passed time reflecting on old memories, time they had spent together on vacation, old inside jokes. Marco started to feel closer to Sheila than he had in a long time. He wasn't sure if it was the force of spending long needed hours together or the knowledge of possible global disaster, but Marco felt *happy*.

In his mind he was at ease, without a care in the world. He felt like a vagabond travelling the country with his hobo wife. Though they hadn't showered in close to a week, she looked beautiful with her frazzled hair tied up in a loose ponytail. It was odd that the crate had actually started to feel like home. He didn't want to leave and face the cruel world, deprived of human interaction.

"I think we've driven past New York by now," Marco said. "Especially since we landed in Manhattan, means we can't see your parents."

Sheila shrugged. She bit her bottom lip. "I don't think I want to. Maybe we will on the way back—if I'm ready?"

Marco hadn't even considered the return trip. How would they get back to Spain? Would they be able to? And most importantly, did they even want to go back? Maybe America *was* in better shape.

"I think we could manage that."

The brakes on the eighteen-wheeler let out a gaseous roar. Marco could hear the unbolting of a lock and the unlatching of a door. The door of the crate then opened and they were swathed in pure sun. Marco felt like a bat. It had been so long since they'd seen the sun it hurt his eyes, like the reflection off of snow.

A man in torn jeans and a black, faded AC-DC shirt stood ogling them. "Last stop," he said with a cackle.

Marco stood from the cot, helping Sheila afterward. They had spent so much time lying down and sitting, that walking had become quite the chore.

"Where are we?" he asked.

"Thirty miles of east of Cincinnati. You're going to have to change trucks. Got Andy waitin' for you by the dumpster," the trucker said, as he jumped onto the ground. Marco followed, hopping into the chill afternoon air. He regretted wearing a t-shirt and no sweater. Though he had one in their bag, he was unwilling to dig for it. The long hours of the trip had drained him completely.

He let out a huge yawn and accepted the bag of necessities, nearly dropping it from the weight. Sheila bent her knees and then jumped onto the pavement. She stretched her arms over her head and arched her back.

"Where ya'll headed to?" the grey bearded man asked.

"California. Going to see my mother."

The man's face tensed up and his eyes turned serious. "I wish you a safe trip."

"Thank you…"

"Mitch." He nodded.

"Thank you, Mitch. I appreciate you taking us this far."

"Yeah, thanks," Sheila chimed in.

"Don't mention it." He smiled, but Marco detected a hint of sadness in the side grin—like he had something to feel sorry over.

Then, the man turned heel and walked toward the cab. He hopped inside and started her up. With one wave of a sun-reddened arm, he was off. Marco and Sheila waved back as the tractor trailer pulled out of the rest stop and took to the highway.

The highways weren't congested like in Spain. In fact, they were empty. He could see the other truck sitting near the curve of the rest stop and when he caught sight of it, the driver honked the loud horn. Marco thought of being a child on a school bus, and how everyone tries to get them to honk their horn, so carefree. He also thought of how children may never again do as such.

"We should go, I guess," Sheila said.

They held hands and walked toward the exhaust-spewing vehicle.

Chapter 25

STRANDED

Andy was a nice but quiet man. He allowed them to sit up front in the cab, unlike Mitch. Though, he couldn't blame the other trucker. He needed to drive an ample distance to make sure he wouldn't be seen letting humans out of the cargo hold. So far they'd driven halfway across the country and it was unexplainably amazing to have the heat on.

Outside of the truck, snow fell in the mountains of Colorado. Marco hated it when they took the steep mountain roads, especially when he could feel the tires sliding little by little. The roads became so narrow at times that Marco could see into the embedded trenches, miles below.

He'd given Sheila the window seat, not for the view, but so that she didn't have to cozy up to the chubby truck driver. It wasn't that she was disgusted by him, like Marco was, but he knew she was un-comfortable. Marco was disgusted for he knew that truck drivers went days and days without showering, fucking hookers in their cabs and masturbating. He could smell the man—like a wet rag, molding in a damp cellar. Then, he thought, do I smell any better? He hadn't a shower in that long either.

The truck crested a steep incline and the hill down was much worse. Andy didn't slow and Marco started to get anxious. He could feel the looseness beneath the tires, the snow stealing the traction from the ground. It felt like the truck was slowly turning to the side.

"Could you slow down, just a little?" Marco asked, feeling Sheila's hand clenched in his own in fear.

"Don't worry. I've driven these roads a million times."

Snow fell past the windshield at a desperate speed. The wipers tried their best to wash the flakes away, but the snow continually picked up. There was almost a blank sheet of white covering their view. The road had all but disappeared, yet Andy was composed. He really did think he was untouchable. Marco thought—one slip up and it would be a wreck.

Andy held the wheel with only one hand. Marco wished he would put his meaty hands at two and ten. He pictured himself taking the wheel in an emergency.

Sheila tilted her head toward the floor of the cab, which was covered in old McDonald's wrappers and crumbs. He knew she was probably reciting a prayer that they would make it safely.

The truck started to slow a little and Marco hoped that Andy wasn't losing his grandiose faith. The front started to tilt, ever so slightly. Then, like a weight pulling a man toward the bottom of the ocean, Marco could feel the trailer swinging forward. It tugged until the truck was an unbalanced letter v and Marco could see the rear wheels in the windshield.

"Make sure you're buckled!" Andy said.

"I told you to slow down!" Marco screamed over the rushing of the humongous vehicle, being dragged through feet of snow, the squealing of the brakes.

"Wait, hold on!"

Marco did as he was told, grabbing the seat with his hand—not only for a brace, but to overcome Sheila's menacing grip. He was glad to have a shoulder belt on in case of a crash.

Andy was pumping the brakes furiously, but with the momentum they had gained Marco knew there was no slowing the train wreck. All they could do was to prepare for the inevitable.

The truck was moving at a breakneck speed, hurtling down the steep incline. The lower they slid, the more visibility there was, allowing Marco a view to the bottom of the hill. There was a car attempting to climb the slope.

"Look out!" Marco screamed, but it was too late. Between swishes of the oncoming car's wipers, he could see a frightened woman lift her hands in the air. The car bent in half on impact and Marco was propelled forward. The seatbelt dug into his chest and Sheila screamed, while still hunkered over in child's pose.

The small Honda went spinning through the thicket of white and then vanished. The truck slid to a stop and Marco started to breathe regularly. It had all seemed to happen in an instant. He wondered if the woman was all right or if she was bleeding out somewhere.

Andy's hands were glued to the steering wheel and he just stared dead ahead, eyes glazed over like a kid in shock. His mouth draped beneath his mustache, open like a tunnel. "I'm sorry," he said. "I should have been more careful—"

"Go check on the person you just hit," Marco said firmly.

Andy ambled out of the driver's side and hopped into the snow. Marco didn't feel bad that the man wasn't wearing a coat. He was reckless and could have (if he hadn't already) killed the woman.

"What the hell did you get us into, Marco?" Sheila asked. "We're out in the middle of a blizzard with no direction and no resources. There's nowhere we could go for help."

Though, he hated to admit it, it could have been equally as reckless going on the trip as staying in Spain. Sure his mother was alone in California, but she was a grown woman. She could take care of herself. Besides— though he hated to admit it, as well—he wasn't even sure she was alive.

"I'm sorry. I've been regretting my decision to make you follow since back on the cargo ship. It was selfish of me."

"You didn't make me *follow*. We are a team, remember?"

He felt a frog pounding in his throat. They were a team, but teams make decisions together, not alone. "We should've stayed at home."

Chapter 26

OIL AND SCALES

As the final passengers boarded the life boat, Portis couldn't help but wonder if it was the right thing to do. Sure, they needed to get away from the machine, but what if there were more of them out there? The larger boat *could* weather the storm better. The small boats would not fare well on the large waves. Then, he thought, sometimes you have no other choices than those into which you're forced.

He climbed into the raft after Mary. With the practiced etiquette of a captain, Portis saluted the ship. He was abandoning it, and with it his title. In the nautical world it brought shame to leave your ship behind, but somehow he thought maybe after all was said and done, he would play it on the safer side and maybe become an accountant or something.

Once all were seated, he started to lower the raft. The ropes squeaked with the descent, and as they passed one of the portholes, Portis could see inside of the ship. He pulled faster. He wanted no reminder of what the vessel had meant to him, how integral it was to his life, how it had become part of his identity. He simply wanted to forget.

The life raft dipped into the water and Portis unlatched the supports. Before he sat, he rubbed his hands along the posterior. He just wanted one last feel…

"I don't know what those aboard think they'll do," Mary said. "There's nobody who knows how to run the ship, even if the engine and thrusters were to boot up."

"I feel sorry for them. From what I gather… nobody will be coming to save them either." He frowned. "Hopefully, they'll grow some common sense and depart."

They looked at each other for a few moments, taking in each other's perception, and then looked away.

"Are we leaving them to die?" Mary asked.

Portis looked at her. "It's possible they'll die. But it won't be on our clock. We can't worry about that. We tried our best to make them understand. Some people you just can't get through to."

He shrugged and took a seat beside her. He knew both of them would worry. It would be impossible to not. He grabbed the oar off the side of the boat. He had a feeling it would soon become his best friend. "Ready?"

"As ready as I ever will be."

"Then stroke on three."

Mary snagged the other oar and hung it over the topsides of the ship. "One, two, three…"

They were the last in line, rowing after a raft manned by two shopping mall security guards. Mary slung her hair over her shoulder and struggled to push the oar through the hectic ocean. Upon noticing her effort and discontent, a male passenger offered to row for her.

"Thank you," she said. "I don't know how long I could do that for. I wouldn't have been much help."

"Might as well give a hand," he said. "My family is on the boat."

The man wore sunglasses around his neck on a rope, hanging over a faded orange shirt. He indicated the woman sitting next to him wearing a sun dress and a less than enthused smile. "This is my wife… Janet."

Portis rowed through a massive wave, which tugged at his oar, nearly dragging it from his hand. The man sat across the aisle and started to row.

"My name' s Fred."

"Pleasure," said Portis between exertions.

Mary had since sat with Janet, and they were talking and laughing very calmly considering the circumstances.

"You two an item?" Fred asked quietly, nodding in Mary's direction.

"No," Portis answered, stunned. "What makes you think that?"

"The way she was watching you…from the moment you stepped on the boat. Could've fooled me."

She'd always been supremely attractive to Portis, but he'd never wanted to blend work with pleasure. It tended to cause friction in the workplace, and he liked to stay professional. However, as he'd been thinking of late, maybe the time was right.

"You're not married, then?" Fred asked.

The question seemed ultra-personal to Portis, something that was none of his business. However, he was never going to see this man again in his entire life.

"No…never got married. Came close once." He thought about Natalie, how she had broken his heart. He'd thought it was true love, but she broke his heart so badly.

"How long have you been married to Janet?"

The man laughed. "Actually…tomorrow is our anniversary. Fifteen years of gold. I love her like I did the day I met her."

He nodded toward a boy and girl sitting closer to the prow. They were blatantly related. "Took the twins with us, felt bad taking a vacation without 'em. Even though it's supposed to be our *special* time."

The boy looked drained and the girl was shivering, wrapping her arms in front of her life vest.

"I wish I would have left them home, safe with their grandparents."

Portis looked at Mary. The man was wishing for something he couldn't change. If there was something Portis wanted in life, it was

141

a change. He didn't want to die alone at sea. There could be no more procrastination. He needed to act.

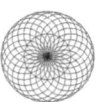

It was just as Pete had feared. A half-hour ahead of the initial machine, there spun another spire. He was surprised that they hadn't seen it before, for in the direction from which they had progressed, the ship sat on the endless horizon like a bird on the surface.

John, one of the bowling alley employees, had seen it first and immediately thought it was another ship. Disappointment had doused the flames of hope once they neared the spire and saw the massive waves forcing outward from the machine. He ordered them to stop rowing and they waved Portis to the head of the procession.

It took a few minutes for them to catch up, floating past the six other vessels, but they did in due time. A hostel of twenty tired faces looked at Pete for guidance.

"We steer around the left. It looks to be spinning clockwise. So, we can catch the wave pushing away from the machine."

Portis looked up from his bench, sweaty and panting. Next to him sat one of the passengers. He nodded in agreement, as if he had a say.

"I'll let everyone know. Be careful, Pete. Stick far outside."

Pete sat back down and began to propel the lifeboat forward. There were more dead aquatic creatures spread around the machine. A shark floated on its side with a giant fish in its jaw. The water was still red, stagnant with slowly leaking blood, despite the field of waves. He pushed dead fish aside with the tips of the oars. There were so many that he considered the oars may not have even been touching the water at all. The smell was overwhelming. It smelt like a rotting fish market.

The wind was exceptionally strong, the closer to the machine they came. Waves lapped against the sides of the tiny capsule, splashing water inside of the boat. Pete's arms gradually started to weaken. His brain felt numb, head permeated by unseen fingers, probing the inside of the cavity. He started to lose control of his muscles, blaming it all on their proximity to the abnormality.

A ripple passed beneath the raft and it dipped far below sea level. Out the corner of his eye, Pete could see a giant wave cresting from the direction of the machine.

"Oh, my God," a woman cried.

The employee, John, asked "What do we do?"

Pete was out of options. "Duck down and cover your heads."

The wave lifted the boat and carried it through the air, against a purple backdrop of twilight. It seemed to dissipate in the air, tipping the boat and tossing its contents of living souls into the Pit of Poseidon. Portis wanted to yell out, to help them, but knew that if Pete wasn't capable, then what could he do?

People plunged into the water screaming and all he could do was watch in horror, as they scrambled to climb back aboard, amongst thousands of dead fish, shellfish, and other crustaceans. They clawed at the sides of the capsized boat, trying to clamber back inside, but all their actions did was to create more friction. The boat rocked back and forth, and Pete tried to calm the panicked passengers through mouthfuls of salted water.

"*Stop trying… to climb back on! If we take turns… there will be weight on there to hold it… steady!*"

No one heeded his feeble warnings, and with nothing else to do, the boat tipped nose down and sank into the murky depths. Pete's head bobbed momentarily beneath the surface as he tried to hold it up, but the scratching voyagers only pushed it farther away.

"*Just float where… you are!*" Pete commanded.

An older woman started to struggle in the strong undercurrent and dipped beneath the water, screaming. "Help! *Help!*"

Portis surveyed the vessel he was guiding. "How many more could we fit?" He asked Fred directly.

As if Fred had already figured it out, he shouted, "At least two… possibly three if we scrunch.

The captain cupped his mouth and shouted, "Two more on every boat!"

Pete splashed toward the struggling woman and grabbed her under the arms. Using a backstroke, he carried her to the closest ship. A few of the passengers carried the crying woman aboard, and then Pete clambered up as well.

He realized that two more to each boat would not be enough. As people swam hard through the waves, disappearing and reappearing, Portis yelled, "One more over here!"

A middle-aged woman with wet spaghetti hair swam weakly to the side of their boat. "Here you go," said Fred, helping her over the gunnel.

She was crying, the tears bleeding into the ocean, once again joining Mother Nature. Her arms were straining to hoist her body over the side of the ship, muscles protruding from the skin. When she came pouring over the side, covered in algae, she flopped onto the deck like a flying fish. Fred opened the duffel bag on the bench next to him and extracted a fleece blanket. He draped it over her writhing body. The wind picked up and she visibly shivered.

"I…" she stammered.

Janet had rushed over, along with Mary. Fred's wife embraced him, while Mary knelt next to the shaking woman. "What dear?" she asked.

"I'm not… cold. When I went under the water, it… something *shocked* me. It felt like a bullet had gone through my stomach. It hurts so *badly.*"

"Mind if I look?" Mary asked, concern washing her face.

The woman slowly shook her head up and down. "Please."

Mary disappeared underneath the blanket, shrouding Portis's vision. Seconds later she said "Everything looks okay."

As she finished, the woman pulled her knees to her chest and vomited. Stringy black vomit poured onto the deck. Janet jumped backwards, looking down at her feet in disgust. Mary rubbed the poor woman's back and she vomited again, thick black and red blood. Pieces of tissue filled the puddle, and spread under the benches. Suddenly, a wave crested and splashed in front of the boat, tossing water over the side and rinsing the deck. The woman coughed and then closed her eyes. Her body froze.

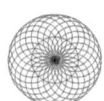

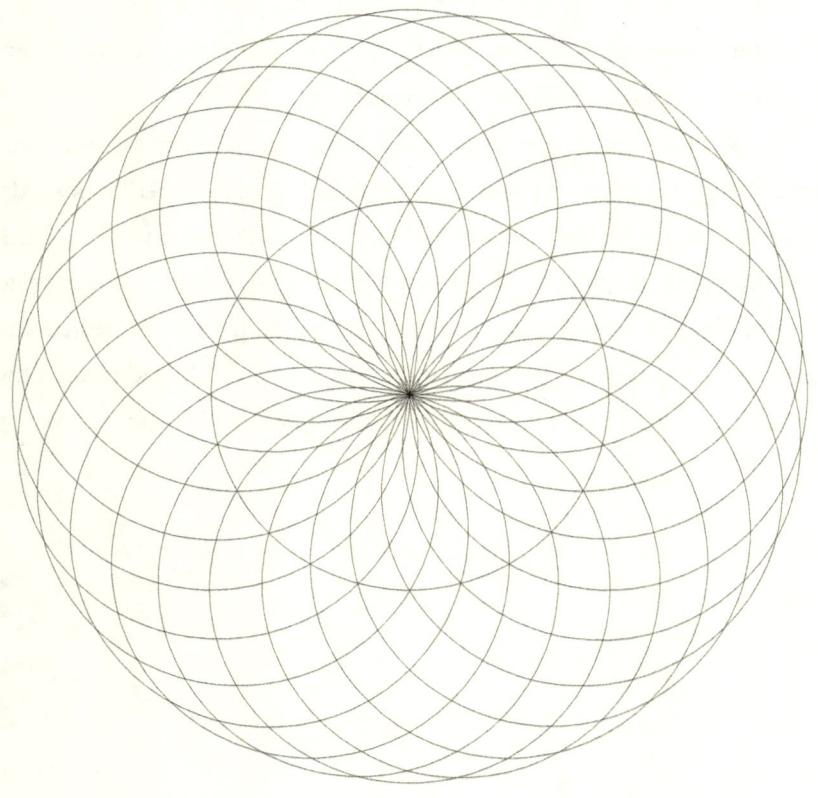

Chapter 27

UNION

The "New World" was an ecosystem of indentured slavery. Sal was forced to pick vegetables and grains day in and day out. They were given exactly eight hours in which to sleep and three twenty minute breaks during which to eat.

Luckily, the food was amazing. However, it wasn't real food. The stuff was genetically modified, developed to grow at rates comparable to that of a maturing insect. A full grown tomato bush took mere hours to form fresh, ripe tomatoes. He'd heard that there were thirteen such chambers, but he'd only been to three.

The heat-emitting lights beat down on Sal, as he used a hoe to even out the soil. The artificial plants could grow in extremely close quarters without dying. One of his shift bosses, Jake, had said the roots are interconnected. Beneath the soil was just a gigantic web of roots, all tangled up and sharing water—a humongous symbiotic organism. He'd only been working four days and already he was beaten.

People had died while working—keeled over and died. Nobody stopped to help and nobody risked a glance, for fear of being shot. Lining the perimeter of the massive chamber were more guards with guns, standing guard and constantly eyeballing the slaves. You were given two warnings if you stopped working. The third was finality. Afterwards, two guards would drag the bodies off. Sal wasn't sure what became of them, but it was odd that soon after, the guards returned with plastic bags full of fertilizer.

Sal was consistently on edge, waiting for a time to conspire, but opportunities never arose. Their sleeping cells literally fit a single ratty cot, and offered barely any walking room. As for belongings, he had only the clothes on his back. He wondered about a shower, but knew that they probably weren't awarded any, seeing as workers weren't expected to last longer than a week at the rough pace of work.

As he used his hoe to even out the dark, fertile soil, Sal counted the guards around the perimeter. There were fifteen, not including however many stood behind him. Judging by the distance of separation between the ones he could see, he concluded that three more were back there. The hoe in his hand was a good weapon, he thought. The small hall leading back to the cafeteria was narrow enough. Also, only two guards escorted the crew. If the front two and rear two workers attacked at the same time—

"Hey! Pick it up!" a guard called to him.

That was warning number one. Sal made it a point to work even harder and faster, despite his weakened muscles. Then, he was struck with a bout of genius, something that rarely came to him. He stuck both hands in the air, as was the gesture.

"Bathroom!"

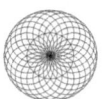

He fiddled around the small bathroom, which reminded him of a gas station utility. They forced him to leave the hoe at his crop patch, along with his collection basket. He checked behind the toilet, behind the urinal, but found nothing. There was a small vent above the toilet stall. He stood on the toilet bowl and tried to pry it off, but failed. His fingernails were too short after chewing them off.

Defeated, he walked to the sink and washed his hands. The warmness felt wonderful, and he took the liberty of washing his face. Brown water filled the sink.

"Hurry up!" someone said through the door.

He was going to turn and leave, but something caught his eye, just at the corner of the mirror. Quietly, he picked at the tiny crack. Another slave must have tried to smash the mirror, probably was heard and was shot. The sound of glass rubbing glass seemed extremely loud in the acoustics of the ceramic lined bathroom. Finally, a small strip fell into his hand. It felt like gold.

The wall of the bathroom was cool, as he leaned against it, beside the door. It lowered his anxiety level. He was planning on waiting for the guard to burst into the bathroom—and then he would attack—but on further thought, pocketed the glass. Even if he killed the one escort and stole his rifle, what about the seventeen others in the agricultural chamber? What about the countless guards outside of the complex, and the security keycard locks?

Propped to the side of the door, his plan changed. He feigned composure and stood off the wall. When he exited the room, the guard looked ready to knock.

"Finally… have some trouble in there?"

"Sorry," Sal said nervously. "I had to take a shit."

"Get going." The rifle poked into the small of Sal's back. He was getting used to the feel of the barrel on his skin.

The walls of the corridor seemed to shrink inward. He could feel the hunk of glass bouncing off his leg, a constant reminder of a near-death decision. He hoped they wouldn't search him. Sometimes the guards pulled random searches, emptying your pockets, occasionally searching bodily cavities if they considered the person suspicious.

Concrete paved way to the giant chamber filled with the freshest air Sal had ever tasted in all of his life. It had a sobering quality to it, compared to the thick pollution of Southern California. Up there, breathing the air was like being stuck inside of a running vacuum's bag.

Upon passing another one of the prisoners, Sal caught his eye. The man couldn't have been over twenty five. He was tall and muscled, also sweating from the extreme heat down there. The look he shot Sal was full of union. It said "Do what you have to, I have your back." The kid then looked down at his garden hoe, back to Sal, and returned to his work. Sal could have sworn he'd seen a wink.

Somehow the kid knew Sal's intentions. How could he not be constantly on the same edge? Surely, none of the others had come to the place in agreement. They had all been tricked or outright captured, he was sure. Every one of them was just waiting for the perfect moment to react, when somebody else would take initiative.

Another woman, distraught filling her eyes, matched his gaze for only a second. She was once a daughter, mother, or sister. Then, her head turned down and she went back to her business, as if Sal were the devil holding her fate. She wasn't quite as prepared as the filthy kid.

These twenty or so peoples' recourse was resting on Sal. If he made a move, they would follow suit. He could feel it in the air, like the lingering of a spent argument. He stealthily slipped his finger into his pocket, hoping the guards couldn't feel the tension. In one liquid motion, he turned, swung his arm like the arm of a windmill, and crouched down.

His hand was drenched in blood. Rapid rifle fire tore through the tall tomato bushes. Sal crawled between the stalks, in the direction he believed the stairs leading to the elevator to be. Once the guard had fallen, Sal rolled to the ground, grabbed the rifle, and searched his body for the keycard. It was tucked into his sock.

A stalk fell near his head and Sal worried that they could see him. Something slammed into his leg with a blazing fire. It burned like a hot coal. He gritted his teeth, trying to hold back a scream. Chances were they were firing at random, but in case, Sal knew he needed to continue moving.

The trek to the elevator would be the most difficult. There was minimal coverage, only a short wall of concrete that Sal didn't think was condensed enough to stop a bullet. As he crawled, he could feel the energy being sapped from his bones. He felt like a skeleton crawling toward his own grave.

Close by, plants were rustling. Sal could see branches shaking. They were searching for him. He rolled onto his back, becoming as small as possible, with his finger on the trigger. The tomato bushes separated and he fired. His ear whistled with the burst.

The kid was shocked, shrouded in gun smoke. He stumbled back, crushing the bushes with a gaping hole in his shoulder. In his hand was a broken hoe, the wooden end jagged and stained with blood. He went to one knee. "What the fuck, man?"

Up close, he looked even younger, maybe in his late teens. Sal thought quickly about going to help him, maybe creating a tourniquet, but decided it would not assist his own survival. He was also shot and hadn't even the time to create his own bandage. Taking the moment to imply one onto the kid would waste his energy, and he wasn't sure what he had left.

The debate was in vain. A guard's bullet cut through the tomato stalks and penetrated the kid's forehead, blasting him from his feet. Sal wasted no more time. He turned in his crouch and charged through the tomatoes. He could see through some of the branches, straight to the concrete. There was also a moving piece of cloth. Bullets ripped and whined into the branches, nearly hitting him. He raised his rifle and fired at the body. To his surprise, it dropped. When he broke out of the bushes, there lay on the ground one of the guards.

With a killer instinct, the guard pointed his gun at Sal. The anonymity of his visor protected his identity. Sal was faster. As the guard choked out a ball of phlegm and blood—courtesy of the bullet hole in his left lung—Sal put a sizzler right through the middle of his face.

Sal crept up the concrete stairwell like an ape, his knuckles nearly brushing the ground. He wasn't trained for this sort of combat, had never served in the military, but felt his confidence gaining with every step. He knew that his fear of death was propelling him forward, rather than his tactical skills. His leg was killing him (literally) and driving him up the stairs at a crawl. His ankle was scratching on the rough ground.

He finally reached the platform to the elevator and swiveled onto his spine, pushing himself backwards toward the door, with his rifle pointed at the stairs. Beyond the guard he had killed, Sal could only see a narrow strip of the chamber, for the wall blocked his field of vision to the right.

Near the front left wall was another dead guard, hunkered against a support pillar, with his chin tucked into his chest. Sticking out of his neck were the prongs of a garden hoe. Sal wanted to check the situation out, but decided against it. Instead, he slid toward the elevator door.

With his back to the wall—parallel to the door—he reached into his sock and unveiled the keycard. Before he could swipe it, the elevator ground to life. He could hear the sliding of the cables inside the shaft. With the strength he was able to muster, Sal crawled past the door to the small cove beyond the entrance. He made himself as tiny as physically possible, a harder target, and readied his gun.

The door slid open and the barrel of a gun protruded a few inches. It fired off a couple rounds and then one of the guards ducked out of the opening. Sal pulled the trigger nervously and missed, hitting the short wall and chipping off bits of plaster. Once the gunfire released, the guard sprinted for the stairs, his gear thunking loudly with his footfalls. Sal pulled the trigger over and over. Before the guard's entire person could vanish, a bullet entered the back of his helmet and he fell forward down the steps like a used and abused doll.

Sal couldn't believe it. He was taking down—

Were they trained soldiers? They certainly didn't fight like trained soldiers. Were they United States Army? Were they cult? An anarchist group? If they were army and the world someday went back to normal, he would be imprisoned. He hadn't gone over the details beforehand.

He heard the elevator door close and he scuttled toward it. After swiping the card in the slot the door re-opened. Sal didn't even have time to raise his gun. Two more guards filled him with metal from chest to face. The last thought he was able to process before he died was that hopefully some of the others would escape.

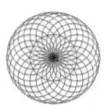

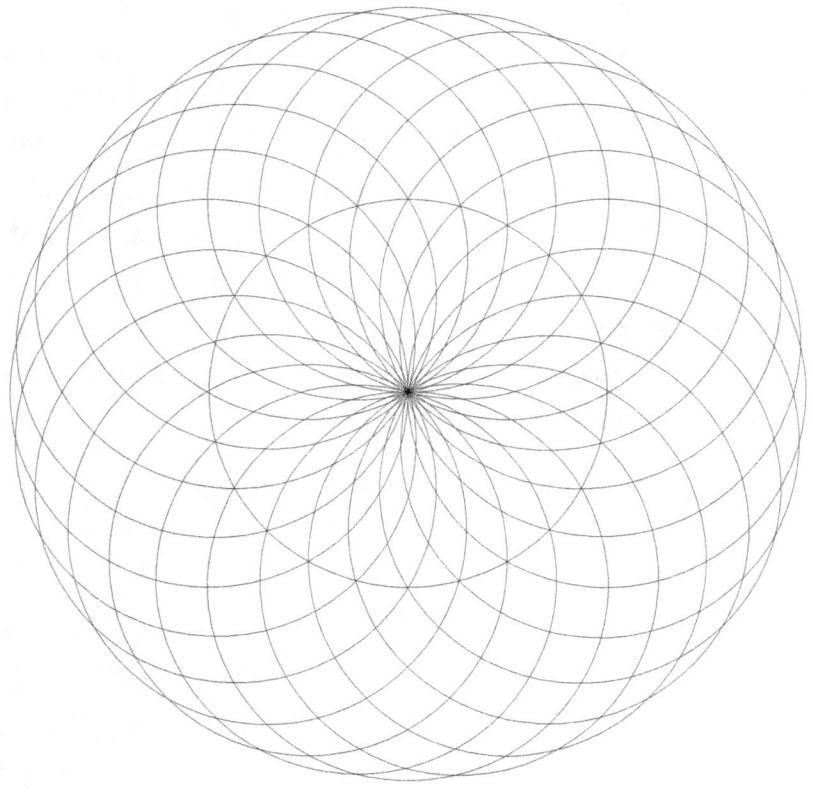

Chapter 28

GODSEND

The cab had turned ice cold in minutes, but Marco couldn't reignite the engine. It revved, but absolutely would not turn over. Andy had been gone, for what Marco counted, twenty minutes. Being out there so long without a coat was a recipe for frostbite and pneumonia. There was no sign of the woman in the car or the pudgy truck driver.

At least the snow had relaxed, he thought. The visibility was still brief, at best.

"You should go looking," Sheila said in between shivers.

Marco was reluctant to step out into the blizzard. For some reason, he'd always been the one to be affected by the cold. If he and his friends went swimming, he was the first out of the water. "I'll go… I guess."

"Be careful, babe. Don't take too long. If you don't see them, get back here."

She kissed him on the cheek. "If you can't find them we'll need to warm up before we go marching through the snow, throw on some extra layers."

"That'll be fun." He walked down the steps carefully—watchful not to slip and crack his head open on the small metal stairs.

It was as cold as he had imagined it to be outside. The wind was fierce. He felt as if the bitter North would tear his skin off. The cold went straight to his bones, making it difficult for his legs to function. Rapidly falling snowflakes required him to squint against an onslaught. Snow fell into his shoes and filled his socks with dampness. He wasn't used to the snow, being a child of Spain and California. To say the least, Marco was out of his element.

As he walked away from the truck, he took a glance back. The truck was barely visible between the falling crystalline. He waved and hoped that Sheila could see him padding away into the unknown.

It made him nervous to think of being stuck in the snow. At least in the woods there are bushes and trees, things to eat. In the world of winter there is only desolation. As far as the eye can see was a layer of pure white, untainted by pollution. To Marco it looked nothing like the snow he'd seen in pictures, of dark brown snow on the side of the road, or massive piles of grey snow in parking lots. The stuff was forged of pure Coloradan white.

Even the air tasted fresher, crisper. It was like breathing in ice. He followed the footsteps of Andy, which were guided by the tracks of the sedan's skidding tires. The further he walked the more apparent became a recognizable ground shaking. It felt like it had that day on the beach. The day the end of the world had begun.

The car was nearly halved when he came upon it. A few inches of frost had already accrued atop the vehicle during its brief stint at a standstill. There was no movement inside, but he noticed through the flakes coating the driver's side window that the passenger's window was smashed out and painted with blood.

Marco stopped. The machine was spinning, much slower than the one he'd seen on television, almost transfixed by the cold. Standing there, he could feel the wind lapping off his cheeks, could almost see it being forged by the machine's edges. Andy was face down in the snow not twenty feet from it—motionless, dead. There was no way he could possibly be so close to the monstrosity and still be alive.

Much like the man in China, Andy's body was melting away. His red Budweiser shirt was uniform with his back, dripping off like a candle. The woman was gone, probably dead like Andy, thrown from the car, maybe even past the machine. There was nothing left there, just unfortunate consequences of a man's poorly decided life.

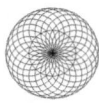

"What did you find?"

Marco shook his head and climbed into the cab. His hair was damp and snowflakes clung to his eyebrows. "They're dead."

Sheila put her head in her hands and started to cry. "Oh, my God. Please, please end this."

Marco wished he had the power to end it, but she wasn't talking to him. She was asking God. Divine intervention was what Sheila had in mind—for God to reach down and press the machines back into the ground, or to pull them out and sling them into the far recesses of the universe. Sometimes Marco wished it worked that way. He wished obstacles in life were as simple to overcome as praying to a deity, but then where would we learn perseverance?

His fingers were numb from being outside. He rubbed them together for warmth, until Sheila took his hands in hers and started to comfort. She always knew when he needed it. Even if he didn't state his displeasure, she could feel it. They had that spiritual connection, which most would discredit as hogwash, and could tell when the other was at odds. Despite the fact that she was probably more uneasy than him, Sheila could stuff it just to reassure Marco that everything was okay, and vice versa.

"We better cover up good," she said through sobs.

"Put everything on. Double socks, triple underwear."

Sheila moved to her knees and dug behind the seat. She pulled out their bag and dropped it between them. Her shirt came off and then her pants.

The last thing Marco wanted to do was take any clothes off. The inside of the cab was like a bakery freezer. His fingers hadn't completely warmed, and the color was still away doing its own thing. Before they departed he needed to at least get the feeling back in his fingers and toes.

Marco started to kick his shoes off. He reached down and peeled one of his drenched socks from his foot. The slightly warmer air stung on his skin. Before he could peel his other sock and shoe off, a small, gentle hand pushed his shoulder into the seat.

She straddled him, kissed his neck. He sat there—spellbound. Usually his mind was in the gutter, but he hadn't thought about sex for a long time. He certainly hadn't thought about it since they'd been home from vacation. His mind was caught up in the machines and the death of a boy named Ernesto, utterly obsessed with them.

Her warm hands slid his jeans down his legs. They hit the floor and absorbed some of the water that had pooled from the bottom of his shoes. She moved her hips against his boxers. He started to sprout. It was the last place he wanted to make it, but he thought they could probably both use the release and the warmth. At the time, anything to take their minds off the world was beneficial.

Her hand found his boxer button and it popped open. His log lay against her crotch. Then, he closed his eyes as she rocked forward, pressing him into her moist passage.

"Just relax…" she said. "Let me warm you."

The first hill was the hardest part. It had taken almost fifteen minutes, by Marco's internal clock, to crest the summit. He could feel the pressure building in his ears, and when they reached the summit, his canals popped.

The weight of the clothes certainly accounted for the expanded time. Though, they kept him warm, they also made him sweat uncontrollably.

At the top Marco had hoped to see a well-lit town, alive and waiting—maybe a crowd out front, lining the roads and cheering their arrival. None of that was there. There were no food or beer tents, just unchallenged ice and mountains. The mountain pass curved left around the perimeter of a peak, and then slanted downhill. Marco thought how much easier it would be to have a dogsled or a snowmobile, and realized why people living in such terrain own them.

Sheila was walking behind him and Marco was forced to slow his step so that she could keep up. He stopped for a moment to catch his breath and allow her catch up time.

"Doing okay?"

She struggled through the high snow. She looked funny with the shirt wrapped around her head as a makeshift hat, hair poking out around her face. "Yeah. My feet are really cold."

His were, too. Regardless of the two extra pairs of socks Marco had put on, snow had found its way into his shoes, re-chilling his toes.

"Hopefully we'll find civilization soon."

Hope—another word that had become obsolete. How can one have hope when everything in life is so inconsistent? Even before the emergence of the machines, Marco thought, was anything consistent? He'd always thought of having his own life regulated, but if you aren't prepared for the future do you really have control?

"Do you think there are any cities nearby?"

"Maybe not cities, but there could be a small town up here. There must be a gas station somewhere along this route."

"Please, God." Again, Sheila was hoping for the help from that big man in the puffy Colorado clouds.

They passed a yellow sign with a squiggly shape on it, meaning the road ahead was curvy. Not seconds later, around a curve, was a sign warning against falling rocks. It would probably be the most dangerous road Marco would ever take.

Looking over the guard rail was like looking straight down into the depths of hell. The giant boulders—pieces of the mountain come undone—lay like discarded children in the valley below, like dead children, like Ernesto. The boulders existed as something separate from the mountain, their own non-thinking entity. Just as the machines that were borne of the Earth acted independently of their mother—wreaking havoc and *murdering*, despite their attachment.

Marco did not want to fall down the disastrous incline, did not want to rest eternally amongst the field of unconscious items. He wasn't ready to become organic matter with them. For the time, he was prepared to remain a sentient human being who could calculate he was far too close to the guard rail, and needed to use a watchful eye to ensure he continued living. He grabbed Sheila's hand and walked her toward the mountain side.

"There's more snow over here," Sheila protested.

"Yes… but we could slip over the edge and fall down that slope."

A sigh permeated the air, thick and resonant with aggravation. "You're too careful sometimes, Marco. Live a little."

Marco laughed. "That's exactly what I'm trying to do." He looked over his shoulder at her, as she started to slack. "What would happen if one of us fell over that guard rail? We don't have cell phones. Nobody is nearby. We'd die. End of story. I'm being practical."

Sheila's voice receded. "What are the chances that one of us slips?"

A smile crept across Marco's cheeks. "What are the chances that giant, nuclear machines pop out of the ground—oh, wait."

Sometimes he was content getting under her skin. He knew exactly how to dig in, right under that first layer of dermis. Then again, she knew how to get him, too. She faded to his left and then stopped.

Marco turned. Sheila was leaning over the guard rail, standing on a slick of ice. "C'mon…" he said. "Stop fooling around."

"I think I could climb down this," she said, putting one leg over the rail.

Her voice seemed to echo over the peaks of the Rockies, reaching to forever.

Marco reached his hand out. "Seriously, I'm not kidding."

"Neither am I," Sheila said, swinging her other leg over the rail. She sat on the cruddy, grey rail staring out at the circling mountains. "I can climb down there. Maybe there's a town down there."

"Actually…" she said, cupping her hand over her eyes. "I think I see lights."

"Sheila."

Her head turned and she kicked her feet carelessly over the open drop. The wind blew hair into her face and sort of hid her, as if she wasn't even there, which—Marco thought—would be the case if she made one false move.

Then, his attention (and hers) was stolen by the unmistakable purring of a car engine. The sound of snow crunching under tires was like music to the ears. Marco sprinted across the ice and gripped Sheila around the arm, hard enough to leave marks. He wanted to not leave the option open for her to climb down the cliff.

"Get off there."

She yanked her arm away. "Don't you *dare* grab me like that, Marco."

He took a deep breath. From around the corner, and washing the side of the mountain, came the warm yellow glow of headlights.

"I'm sorry. Please… get off there."

She raised an eyebrow and channeled her energy into reversing off the guard rail. "Much nicer don't you think?"

Marco bit his tongue as he held her hand like a princess and escorted her away from the cliff. What came around the corner, then, was a beat up Chrysler, riding on hubcaps and snow chains. Rust outlined the bottom of the car's frame like burnt crust on toast. The brakes squeaked as it rolled to a slow stop.

Inside, Marco could see an older woman with dark brown hair. She struggled to roll her window down with a chubby arm. When he could see her face it lightened his heart. She had a rosy complexion and doe eyes. Her name could have been Janine or Noreen.

"Well, what are y'all waiting on—summer? Hop inside!"

Chapter 29

THEY SPEAK

In the dream, Marco was in the forest behind their home in Spain. He was walking farther into the branches in a foggy haze. His gait was slow and everything around him seemed to be moving—if not at a steady pace, then very slowly—in concert. Branches waved like arms and vines reached, desiring to choke him.

As usual in a dream state, his feet moved without the knowledge of where he was going. He never examined his own body and seemed to be peering through someone else's eyes and into his own set. The soil was alive with the fervor of millions of insects, crawling over his shoes (not that he looked, but he could feel them), and gradually climbing his pants leg.

Fresh trees and bushes seemed to take root spontaneously, filling the forest to a point of no admittance. The path he was on became wholly apparent, outlined by the impassable lines of brush, which reached but never contacted. The route began to drift upwards. As it did so, the vegetation started to bustle with the obvious disruption of animal life.

Marco's dream-self did not falter, despite his subconscious plea to turn back in fear. He could not control his inner thoughts, could not control where his brain wanted to bring him. Inside the beech trees and holly bushes, eyes started to appear, humanly eyes. They focused solely on his journey.

Ahead a pair of the eyes—which were yellow and low to the ground, maybe waist high—crept free of the prison of green. A skinny creature, thin like an anorexic, stepped gracefully into his path. It wore dark brown slacks that looked hand-sewn and an ivy green vest with nothing on underneath. The skin draped over its bones was thick and light brown, like the bark of a tree. Entranced, dream-Marco followed as the thing walked backwards in front of him.

It didn't quite skip, but moved with the finesse of a ballet dancer, lifting one foot before the other. From the leather belt around its waist, a small silver flute slid out. The sound which emitted was the most beautiful music Marco had ever heard in his entire life. Not a tone went astray, a pitch never broken, and absolutely none of it corrupted by the blues of society. It was a lightened song.

He felt weightless and pure, and despite the fact that he knew it to be a dream, whole for the first time. For then, he felt belonging to something bigger, brighter, and more fantastic than his human mind. He felt as if his body had transcended the physical world.

The imp led him forward with a gentle wave of the hand. Following the imp's lead, other creatures started to appear from the brush, lining the sides of the path like a gauntlet. They looked like pleasant creatures, welcoming even though they weren't smiling or showing any proper emotion. However, his focus was on the sprite in the middle of the path, guiding him up the dirt hill. Above the arch of the hill, Marco could see the top of one of the machines. It spun in slow circles, not in the usual fashion, but more like the spire from the mountains.

At the top of the hill, dream-Marco finally stopped. The imp started to dance circles around the obscure machine, coming so close it was impossible. The rest of the forest dweller's brethren began to pass Marco on his sides, each one glancing briefly at his face in passing. They crowded around the tall shaft, staring at him, quietly swaying.

He felt the insects crawling over his pants legs once more. Finally, his dream-self looked down. Thousands of bugs, with human faces, were climbing his body. He began to sink into the soil. He could feel the dirt passing, his body parts being pushed on. It felt like a sea beneath him, pulling him down, accepting him.

The soil reached his waist and the forest dwellers moved toward him, circling his body. The one with the flute sheathed its instrument and put its small hands behind its back. They watched in fascination as Marco sank into the Earth. He could feel the dirt encompassing his neck, harder to breath. The bugs tickled his face and dirt filled his ears, along with the screams of the bugs.

Beneath, the ground the Earth was reverberating. His body quivered. As insects started to crawl over his eyes—he could see feelers and wings—the destructive spire began to sink along with him.

His eyes flapped open, filled with glorious sunshine that had somehow broken through the masks of clouds that were in the sky. Marco lifted his head. Sheila was asleep in the front seat, her head leaning on the passenger's side window. A pair of light brown eyes regarded him in the rearview mirror.

"Finally up?"

Marco let out a giant yawn. "Yes… I feel rested."

"I should hope so," the woman, whose name turned out to be Marianne, said. "You slept a good thirteen hours."

"Jesus, where the hell are we?" Marco asked, looking out the window into more mountains that were green and filled with desert brush. He realized he was sweating from the sun pounding through the windows. It was probably what had woken him.

"About an hour west of Reno. One more and we'll be in Sacramento."

Marco leaned forward and placed a hand on Sheila's shoulder. She jumped and lifted her head. When she turned and looked at Marianne, she jumped again, as if she had forgotten they had hitchhiked halfway across the country with a stranger. Maybe she was sleeping the entire time, too, he thought.

Her hand found his and squeezed. He was sure that she could feel it was his. Their hands always fit together perfectly, like they were two pieces of a puzzle and were meant to join. When Sheila saw the surrounding landscape, she asked "Where are we?"

"Almost to Sacramento."

"What?" She spruced up and sat Indian style. "You drove us all the way to California?

Marianne chuckled. "I told you I would take you West."

Sheila shook her head. "You really shouldn't have. It's too much, Marianne."

For a moment she took one of her hands off the steering wheel and gave a relaxed wave. "Don't fret. I've always wanted to go to California, just never had the money. I figure... if it's the end of the world, I might as well see the West Coast before I die."

It was surreal to think of the end of the world, to think that one minute there would be a globe of living beings and vegetation, the next there would be nothing but a giant rock floating through space. He wondered if that had happened to Mars. If so, what had challenged God to ruin the planet? Did he decide that whatever creatures he had created to inhabit the planet were incorrect? With the human race so young, compared to the lifeline of the universe, was he just realizing that humans were a mistake and it was their time to go? It didn't feel like just the right time to Marco.

"How long are you planning to stay?" Sheila asked.

Marianne shrugged. "I don't know. If it's really warm there, I may not leave!"

"Probably depends on the situation," Marco said. "I have a feeling that California is in a world of trouble. It's too commercial out there."

"Well, at any rate… I'll be headed for the ocean. I want to take a swim in the Pacific."

A car passed in the other direction on the highway. Marco looked into the window of the red Jeep. It was filled to the brink with luggage, plastic bags, and furniture. A very frightened-looking man was driving. He wondered where the man was headed. Was he going on a search for family as well, hoping to connect with them maybe for the final time? Or was he going somewhere he'd never been, like Marianne was planning?

Marco had always wanted to go to Egypt, and Sheila always to Paris. Maybe they wouldn't ever get there. Maybe they would never fulfill any of their bucket list desires, like skydiving and bungee jumping. At least they'd accomplished one of them—driving across America. He wished that they'd been awake for it.

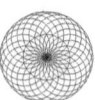

S acramento was not what Marco remembered it as, but that's what happens when a city is riddled by earthquakes. He could tell from the gaping cracks in the pavement and rubble constituting the plots where houses had once stood. When they came upon his mother's house, Marco was grief-stricken to see that there were only pieces of timber and roofing, forming a pile of debris.

Marco started to bite his fingernails—something he hadn't done in years—once Marianne pulled out front of the curb and idled the engine. It was difficult to find the house, considering there weren't many landmarks by which to abide. Luckily, Marianne's map had been semi up to date, for there was no GPS in the car (not that it would have worked anyhow).

He hopped out of the car as fast as possible, his feet barely touching the pavement, before he was darting over the sidewalk and the front lawn. Once he reached the edge of the mound, Marco started to search through the hunks of siding, broken walls, and supports that he couldn't lift. Grabbing one side of a wall, Marco gripped and lifted with all his anguish. He felt his muscles strain, but it wouldn't budge. Frustrated, he dropped it the inch he had lifted it.

He stood atop the pile of house he had half grown up in, panting like a dog and on the brink of tears. He couldn't rip his mind from the idea that his mother was lying dead beneath his feet. Looking around at his old neighborhood, he wondered if there were any other dead beneath their houses. Where the hell were the emergency services? He hadn't thought things would be that bad in America.

Then, he realized the lack of traffic on the route to Sacramento. For most of the time he had been spacing out (or sleeping), thinking of a way back to Spain, not quite noticing how few vehicles were on the road.

As he looked around the neighborhood his heart dropped in his chest. There was no one in sight. Most of the houses were decimated to the ground or falling in on themselves. One of his neighbors' houses, the Patterson's, was actually collapsing into the Earth, as if it had fallen into a sinkhole. Then, something caught his eye, far beyond the Patterson household—a small speck of a man, rummaging in a destruction site.

Marco hurried through the scraps of house, sprinting past the idling car. One of the windows buzzed down with his passing and Sheila asked "Where you going?"

He didn't slow or look over his shoulder, just yelled into the quiet afternoon air. "There's somebody over there!"

The ground was rumbling, enough that his progress was slowed and he tripped sideways. He didn't fall, simply lost his balance a little. Obviously, there were still some aftershocks happening. Marco realized that the earthquakes must not have occurred too long before, or there were just so many of them that they continually were destroying the geology.

The man heard the approaching footsteps, because he looked up from his undetermined and uninspired debris shuffle. A look of concern spread across his face, and he started to back off.

"What are you doing, man?"

Marco slowed, not wanting to step into the wreckage or alarm the man any further. He recognized his old neighbor. "Mr. Breckenridge?"

He squinted through circular spectacles, working the age progression over in his mind—placing facial hair, stretching Marco's cheekbones, hardening his features. When he pulled all the features into one human specimen, he need not ponder over why Marco was there, or what he could possibly want. Breckenridge spit out "They're at the school."

Marco was out of breath. "What happened?" he asked.

"There was a series of natural disasters. First, there was a mudslide and then an earthquake. As you can see, what was left of the city after the mudslide was taken out by the quake."

Just as Breckenridge said, the ground was coated with dried mud and dirt that Marco had not noticed before. It was caked onto and into everything. The pavement looked like a dirt path at a Four-A show. "So my mother's all right then?"

Breckenridge sniffed as if he smelt something awful. "Yes… she's okay, a little shaken up, but otherwise all right." The sun glinted off the glass of his spectacles. It was starting to get hotter.

"Weather has been fluctuating, too," Breckenridge said. "Hot then cold. I feel like I'm living in New England again, for crying out loud." He tilted his head down, as if reminiscing on better days.

"Do you want to come with us?" Marco asked the somber fellow.

Breckenridge pushed his lower lip over his upper, and kicked a board apart even more. "Nah… you remember Sandy?" he asked, once again making eye contact, trying to compose something of a smile on his face.

Marco nodded. "Yeah, of course."

The neighbor took a deep breath and pushed his hands into his pockets. In the instant, he reminded Marco of a kid, upset from dropping his ice cream cone. "She's dead…" he said, almost nonchalantly, as if it was the most natural thing in the world.

Maybe it was, thought Marco, birth and death being more natural than anything in the world. Both derived only from our ancestors' exposure to this world, or spoiled and wasteful existence. Other things are made by humans, but life… life is the one natural experience that cannot be exactly replicated or reproduced. Yet, something wholly unnatural (and possibly manmade) had brought on the death of Sandy.

"It wasn't her time, Marco. She was a good woman. I should be the one under this rubble." The man sniffled and wiped at his right eye.

"I'm sorry, Mr. Breckenridge."

He shook his head and grimaced. "I hate when people say that, always have. Manners, it is they say. Condolences—like it'll raise the dead, or make me forget. I don't want to forget… I want to remember."

He hadn't meant to offend him, only (like Breckenridge had said) offer his sympathy. Marco knew firsthand, from when his father had died, how plastic the phrases can sound. How cookie-cutter phrases like "sorry for your loss" can start to sound, after hearing it a thousand times. How it can drive the dagger deeper with the constant reminder, rather than pardon your tears and pain. He almost apologized again, but caught his tongue—better to allow the man silent grievance.

Instead, he said "We're headed out, then. If you need anything, you know where to find us."

His words sat in the air, creating a few awkward moments where he wasn't sure if he should return to the car or wait for a response. Behind him, Marco could hear the Chrysler's engine rumbling. Marco started to turn toward the car, keeping his peripherals on the beaten man.

He said, "Stay safe, Mr. Breckenridge."

A tiny frown curled on his face. "I'm going to find somewhere nice to bury her when I find her… away from these fucking machines… away from this Godforsaken civilization."

Marco assumed there was nothing left to say, and felt it appropriate for his neighbor to have the final word. Slowly, he opened the door and climbed inside the back seat. He placed a hand on Sheila's shoulder, like he always did. He just wanted to feel the warmth of her skin, to know she was still there.

Marianne asked, "Where to?"

He looked around and noticed a stop sign leaning on a forty-five degree angle, the post rusted from the Earth's natural elements—a man-made sign that *we* put there, not able to withstand the cruel torment of unrelenting winds and water.

"Take a left at the stop sign."

He wondered where Breckenridge would go. For it seemed that man's destruction was everywhere, spread like butter over the world's burnt landscape. It was inescapable.

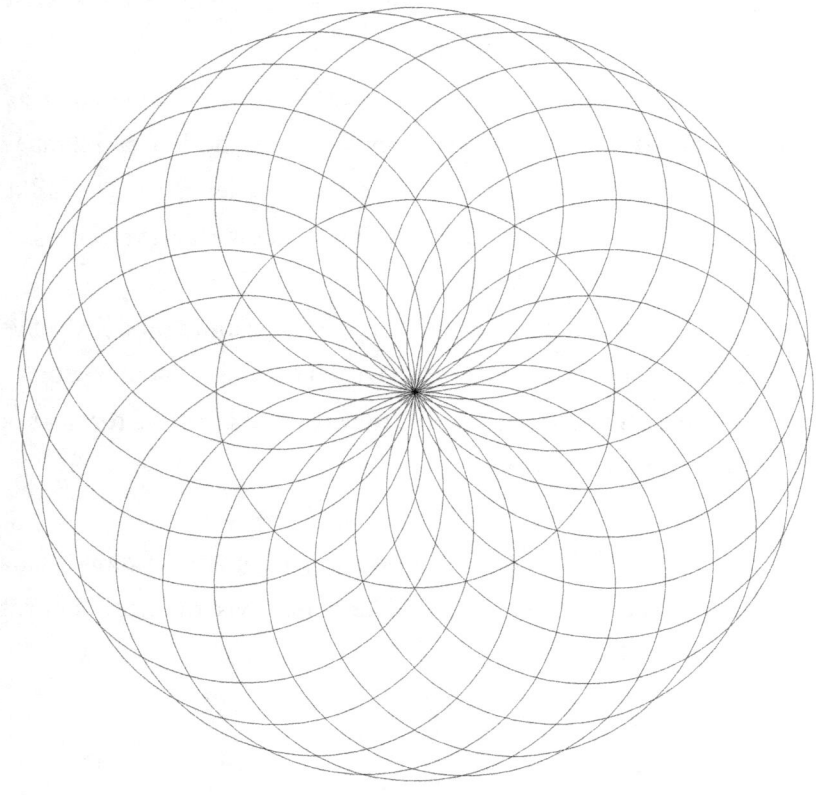

Chapter 30

PARADISE, AT LAST

Yet another boat became a victim to the disastrous spinning of the nearby spire, but it was not from indirect contact.

Portis had taken the lead and Pete followed up the rear. After packing the ships (with the overboard passengers) like containers of sardines, the vessels edged cautiously around the left side of the machine. It spun slowly, like a merry-go-round, in the wind, but there was a constant battle against the thirsty whirlpool surrounding it. One of the ships must have come too close and Portis heard Pete yell, "Pull left! Pull left!"

There were screams and a sound like two balloons rubbing against each other, but much louder. One of the rafts had succumbed to the machine's draw and was pulled in. The raft exploded and the passengers were being spun around the unrelenting monster. Arms flailed above the water, searching for traction. Bodies bounced off the spire, entwining with one another in a gruesome blend of human flesh.

Portis had to cover his mouth once the red began to spread around the base perimeter of the machine. The overboard people grabbed at armfuls of things that weren't there, called out for help, trying to swim away from the circular death trap. Limbs began to vanish beneath the surface, tugging handfuls of seafood with them. The skin was bubbling on the overboard passengers' faces and their limbs melting away, leaving pieces of skin floating alongside the dead fish.

Pete was rowing with all his might. Portis could see his biceps tensing into hardened balls. He wanted to lend a helping hand, as always, but for once Portis knew it best to be selfish. The more people who tried to help, the more congested the area would become, and the more lives would be lost.

Finally, he stopped rowing, concern flooding the other passengers' faces. However, the raft continued to drift closer to the machine, as if magnetized. Pete did not try to stop its movement, but started to strip off his shirt. The captain stood, making the boat he was on start to rock and the other passengers start to complain.

Portis cupped his mouth. "Pete! Don't you do it! That's an order!"

Pete glanced absently at Portis, rotating his shoulders in preparation, and then leaped into the frigid Atlantic. He moved over the rough waves with ease, a world class swimmer, but Portis knew he was going to die of disgrace. The machine would not stop for him. Heck, it may even pick up speed, the captain thought, with the wholesome indulgence of Pete's strong soul. When Pete wants to do something, there is absolutely no stopping him.

He grabbed ahold of a teenage girl, whose face was missing bits of skin—her cheeks nearly see through to the bone—and tossed her over his shoulder. For a moment, he was nearly sucked under, but adrenaline took over and Pete was able to drag her to safety. Four more times he did this— bringing two more women, a young boy, and a fat man back to his own raft.

Just as Portis began to think that Pete was going to live, he saw in his friend's face, a lapse of energy, like he had decided five lives were well worth his own. He vanished beneath the murky waters. Before his head could fully disappear, he managed to spit out one last word.

"Row!"

He hadn't expected for them to find land so fast, but it was like a Godsend after two days on the open ocean, when they landed on the shore of an island. In their travels, they had come across four more of the spires.

The first carried oil up from the floor of the ocean, which coated the sides of the boats and made the ocean look for miles like a gigantic inkwell.

The next two were within one hundred feet of each other and spun much faster. The momentum of the spires spinning in opposite directions sent giant waves down the center. It took hours just to circle around them, unsure of if they were even going in the correct direction, toward land. Portis had a pocket compass, but the hand only teetered back and forth like a drunken mouse. Five rafts were capsized trying to get around the dual machines, only three passengers from the vessels surviving the bout.

Just as it was a Godsend to see land, it was as if the devil had risen from Hell once they saw the machine on the shore of North Cay. Portis had hoped these machines were only in the ocean, but no such luck. It was dug into the beach like an umbrella of an annoying beachgoer, blocking your view of the ocean and completely unwilling to move.

The area around it was sunken, and the sound of sand being sucked into the crevice was ceaseless and disheartening. Palm trees lay across the beach, a vision of dead paradise. It was most certainly not the cruise the passengers had paid for, but alas, Portis had in the end delivered them to the Bahamas.

They settled into one of the yacht clubs, where the zombie-like owners offered them fresh coconuts and papayas. The fruit was bland, but severely satisfying. A dinner was being prepared of fresh slayed boar and fried plantains when Portis stole into Mary's room. Though, her back was turned, she didn't flinch or jump when he placed his hand on her shoulder. They had been through too much to be scared by the soft and surprising feeling of a gentle hand.

He whispered, "I love you, Mary."

She turned and brought her lips to his. They kissed for what seemed like eternity, salty tears mixing in their dehydrated, but passionate kiss. To Portis, hers were the driest lips he had ever tasted, and also the softest and most suitable.

When they broke, she said, "I love you, too. I've been waiting for this for so long."

He held her in his arms, glad that he had finally taken the step. From henceforth, he vowed to live with no regrets, like Pete always told him. He would cherish each moment he was breathing and live to the fullest, for there is not a moment to waste.

Being a captain did not define him, and though it would take a long time, he knew with Mary by his side he could move on and not dwell on the lost passengers. With every loss, there comes a gain. He had learned that from a very dear friend, whom he could never possibly forget.

Chapter 31

HARDER TO BREATHE

His mother looked brought to malnutrition. Never before did she have a belly, but seeing her after such a long time period, her stomach had bulged and her limbs thinned out like spaghetti. Where once she had eaten solely home-cooked meals, her menu had been reduced to highly preserved foods, chock full of high-fructose corn syrup and ingredients only listed as acronyms. Marco promised that when they returned home he would cook an exquisite meal, whichever type of food she desired.

After performing numerous test flights, the American military considered flights out of the country to be safe, but held the doors to immigration closed. Civilian aircraft weren't permitted to fly, but the Air Force was offering flights for veterans, dual-citizens, and tourists leaving the country a method of departure for cheap. The government wanted as many people out of the country as possible. Seeing as Marco, his mother, and Sheila all had dual-citizenship, it was simply a matter of finding the closest air base.

Marco's father had served in the military for fifteen years, but Marco would never join. Not only did he not possess the gall to kill another human, but he didn't feel that wars were fought for just causes any longer. The Civil War had its purpose, the World Wars had their purposes, but now—he figured—countries fought over things that were none of their damn business. Yet, his father's years of serving had brought him, his wife, and his mother back to Spain. So, he couldn't complain too much.

Montejo de la Sierra was very much the same once they escaped from Madrid. Nothing had really changed—except for at the summit of the mountain there was a huge hole, where the machines wind or radiation had downed trees and brush. This brought back memories of Ernesto, and how the boy's mother had been completely destroyed by the occurrence. Marco felt a pang of guilt that he should be alive with his mother, while somewhere in the village there was a grieving mother, missing her young child.

His own mother was resting after the very long trip. Her ankles were hanging over the arm of the couch and she had a red cotton washcloth over her face. She had regained some color, but was still looking rather frail and deathly.

Sheila was doing the dishes, the running water and clinking of glass a beautiful reminder that they were home.

His mother shifted so that her head was angled enough to look at him.

"You found a very nice wife, Marco. She will take care of you."

The way she said it implied that his reason for helping her back to Spain was to protect and care for him. In reality, he just wanted his mother living within a safe distance, so that he could be assured of her safety.

"I'm glad you came with us, Mom. With you here I feel much better. Soon you will, too."

Her smile reminded him of his life as a young boy, when he would get home from school and she would hug and kiss him. It fulfilled his separation anxiety.

"As am I. I never should have waited so long to return to Spain."

She moved one arm above her head, propping it up. "It's my home… I belong here. Without your father…"

Her head drooped a bit, like she had never truly gotten over him. "I've always felt out of place there. Sometimes it felt like home, when I closed my eyes and dreamed, but never quite right. Never quite."

Marco rocked in the recliner, lifting the footrest. He reached into the chair's console, grabbed the remote, and flipped on the television just for shits and giggles. The screen was filled with snow.

"Will it ever get back to normal?" Marco asked.

His mother shrugged and rolled onto her side to face him. "I hope it's like every other happening… people talk about it for an unusual amount of time, and then it sort of drifts away. It becomes forgotten. At least we can try to co-exist if they don't leave."

Her word choice had been well planned (co-exist), as if they were alive and thinking. Marco thought then, who's to say they aren't? It didn't pardon their presence, but hearing his mother say that she believed things would run their course was very comforting, even though it might not be true. Yet, she did tend to have a marvelous insight.

When Marco awoke the morning after, his first mission was to head to the café and check on Manuel. It had been too late when they'd arrived the night before, pushing on eight o'clock, the time of night Manuel typically retired to the bedroom.

He walked into the establishment and was puzzled to not see the skinny bald man behind the counter, but Solzhein. It was rather amusing for a Special Forces agent to act as a barista. Marco nodded and offered a forced wave and smile.

"Hello, Marco."

"Hey… where's Manuel?"

"He's at home. I'm his coverage for the time being. Bad asthma attacks he's been having. They've bedridden him for the better part of a week."

Marco thanked Solzhein and exited the café, the bell jangling on his departure. He wondered how Solzhein had become Manuel's replacement, what set of circumstances would have conveyed him into that position. Hell, Nino would have been a better choice. Then, he remembered that Ana was Manuel's niece. She had been acting very chummy with Solzhein, just before the search party had gathered. He shook it off. Either way, what really mattered was Manuel's health.

The quaint two-story home came into sight, small dead bushes alongside the house, fading siding. It looked dead itself. No lights were on, but Marco barged through the front door uninvited. Ana stood off the couch, looking completely frightened. She sprung into defense mode, but seeing Marco, visibly relaxed her squared shoulders.

"Is he okay?" Marco asked.

"Yes. The doctors have him on bedrest. They don't want him moving around at all."

"That's good." He took a breath, felt his heart start to slow down. "So, Solzhein had been in charge of the café?"

Marco wasn't sure, but he thought Ana blushed.

"He graciously offered to assist my uncle with running the business."

Through the floorboards above, Marco could hear Manuel hack. It happened for a few moments, and then he went silent. Marco gazed upon Ana, wondering if either of them should answer his distress.

"He's fine. I've had him under watchful eye."

After a few beats, she said, "Nobody else would help with the café, you know. People are scared to come out of their houses. They think it's the apocalypse or something."

It's what had happened in America, Marco recalled. Eventually people stopped going to work and businesses began to close. They were lucky to get out of the country when they did, while gasoline was waning, but available. Food supplies were almost depleted. There was mass crime and looting. Schools had even closed their doors.

"Mr. Rivera shut his farm off to the public. He doesn't sell grocery at the market anymore... barely anyone does. Phillip had to answer a call—ten of Rivera's sheep were stolen two weeks ago."

For somebody to steal Rivera's sheep was unheard of in Montejo. It was such a close-knit community, he couldn't even fathom who would commit such a crime. Certainly nobody he had ever conferred with in the village.

"Did he determine who stole them?"

"Not yet. He's still working on it."

"Well I hope he finds them and puts them away."

"He will. He won't rest until justice is served."

An awkward silence hung in the room for a minute, long enough for both parties to feel uncomfortable and try to talk at the same moment.

"Is—"

"He's—"

"Go ahead," Marco said.

"He's doing fine if you want to go up."

"Okay. I won't bother him for long."

As he walked up the steps, he could hear Manuel's heavy wheezing, traveling down the hallway. It sounded as if he was gasping for his life, trying to inhale every spare molecule that his constricted lungs could indulge upon. The door whined open and Marco was granted with a horrific visage.

The room was darkened, the shades drawn on both windows, and an air purifier hummed in the corner. Manuel, or what was left of him, lay in the large bed with the comforter pulled up to only his waist. Covering his face, arms, and chest was a layer of sweat. His eyes were closed. He looked at peace.

Marco wasn't sure if he should speak or softly sit, he was fearful of scaring his friend and sending him into another asthma attack. So, he walked with heavy feet, hoping Manuel would hear his footfalls. The old man's wrinkly lids peeled slowly open, not afraid in the least.

"Marco…" Manuel wheezed, sounding like a deflating balloon—a once full of life parade balloon, popped at the end of an exasperated route. "How long have you been here for?"

"Not long," Marco said, sitting on the side of the bed. He felt comfortable taking Manuel's hand and holding it, without feeling the least bit gay. "We got in last night. I would have come sooner, had I known. It took so long to get to Cali—"

"I know, I know. Family comes first, always." He said it in a way that suggested he wasn't as important to Marco, not part of his family. However, Marco hadn't felt emotion for another male since his father had been alive. Uncle Ricky lived so far away, and he'd only met Sheila's father a handful of times, never allowed the opportunity to build a relationship.

"You *are* my family, Manuel. I'm sorry for leaving. I wish I could've been here."

"I understand, my son. You don't need to explain yourself." He hacked a wet cough. Pieces of spittle plopped onto the red comforter, filled with green and yellow phlegm.

"You can't always be there for everyone, Marco."

Manuel was right, but it was part of who Marco was as a person. He tried so hard to please everyone. "How are you feeling?"

"Better today. Last evening my chest seized up and the doctor rushed over. He had me on a breathing machine all night."

"Did he tell you why it's acting up so much right now?"

Manuel took as deep a breath as possible, draining him. Marco needed to stop asking questions, he realized. The man need not be speaking long winded phrases. He really needed to rest his lungs.

"Doctor Ramirez says that since the machines surfaced…" he took a calculated breath, "the air has thinned out. Oxygen levels have dramatically dropped. You may have had difficulty breathing and not even known it."

"Do you think the Earth is dying, then?"

"I'm not sure it's dying. Even if it was, what could we really do? In man's short time he has done irreversible damage to the planet. Our generation is suffering the consequences."

It was one of the most accurate statements Marco had ever heard in his life. Man was continually sucking Earth's resources dry. If it wasn't coal, it was oil. If it wasn't trees, it was metal. They were—and he included— destroying a beautiful thing, a thing that could neither defend itself nor recover independently. Concrete was slowly creeping through the trees.

"I had a strange dream the other night," Manuel said in between breaths. "I was walking through the woods, and this... sprite came to me."

Marco had a feeling he knew where the story was going. There was a pang in his heart. Were there coincidences, or was there some unspoken and unseen blueprint?

"It was awful, Marco." Manuel shook his head and closed his eyes. His chest labored up and down.

"One of those dreaded spires drove up through the ground... it turned the poor sprite into putty. Blood shot over my face and body—I could swear I tasted it. When I awoke, I was having an asthma attack."

Though, it was slightly different and more gruesome than his, Marco viewed it as much the same. The Spirit of the Wild was speaking to them. Who knew how many others had dreamt the same sequences. Had they backhanded the forebodings, gone on living, dismissing the visions as just a beautiful or horrific picture derived from their imagination? Were they living in typical human ignorance? For Marco, it was a revelation.

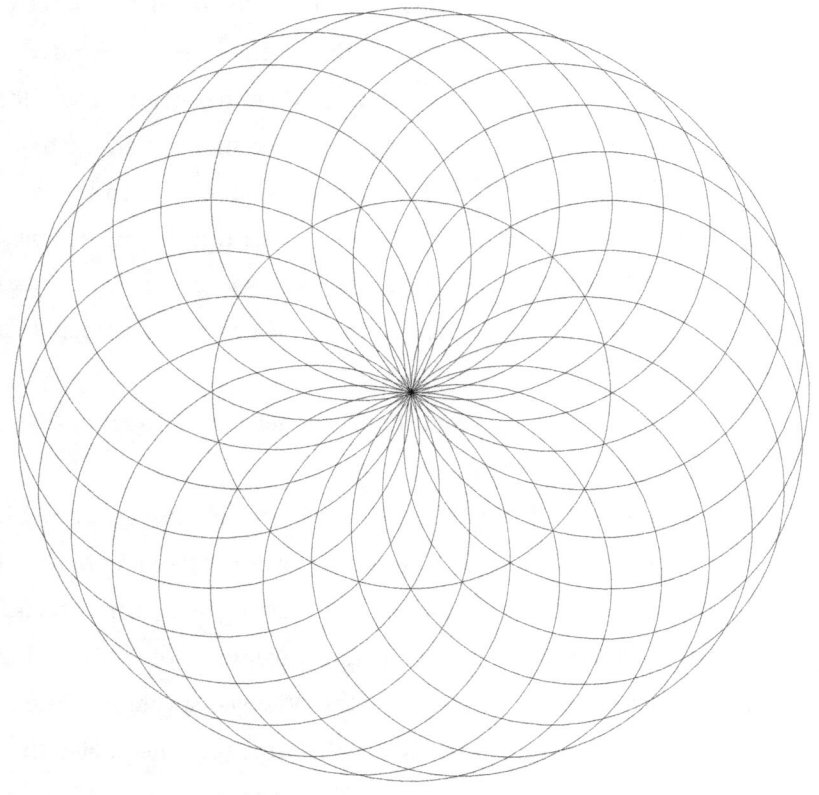

Chapter 32

ACCEPTANCE

Marco woke with the flavor of blood in his mouth, could taste it like a blend of sour tomato sauce and copper. It was almost the exact dream Manuel had experienced, and it was equally dreadful as he had explained. Sweat was dripping down his cheeks and it was difficult to breathe. He felt like he'd climbed to the peak of Mount Everest and taken off his oxygen mask. Beneath him, there was also a puddle of sweat, drenching the mattress and comforter.

Sheila slept next to him, peacefully as usual. She was flipped on her side, body inflating every few seconds, moonlight basking her hair in a reflective white. He slipped out of bed, doing his best not to wake her, and kissed her forehead very lightly. At the window overlooking El Chapparal, the forest which had been the inspiration for the dreams, Marco pulled the curtain aside.

The trees sat tranquilly rustling in the wind. The branches swayed in even, almost coordinated movements, a very endearing dance that made Marco want to join. His face drew closer to the window pane, his breath fogging the glass. He looked upon the summit of the mountain where the machine had formed a clearing, where Ernesto was flung to his death, and close to where the three Legionnaire agents had perished. He thought of Manuel and his gradual zombification, how it was only a matter of time before his good friend was merely a scrap of flesh resting beneath the blankets. Then, he thought of his mother and Sheila, the two women for whom he cared more deeply than his own life.

How long, he wondered, would it be before the air was no longer breathable? How long before the radiation started to show its gruesome effects? Was God trying his chosen ones, or disposing of them? Were the machines a warning, or had Earth's self-destruct button been pressed?

Marco snuck from the bedroom after kissing Sheila softly on the head, with the thoughts fresh in his mind. He paced through the kitchen, regarding the appliances, wondering how long before the electricity turned off. Would people resort to cannibalism once the meat spoiled? As he passed through their front door, he hoped the click wouldn't wake Sheila. She would need her rest.

His mind carried him toward El Chapparal, toward the people of the forest with flutes and whistles. He thought of the fables Manuel told him in which the spirits entranced humans into the woods and turned them into snakes and snails. Maybe Ernesto is out there, he thought, sliding through puddles or swallowing mice and insects.

The spirits had spoken to him, and who-knew how many others. He walked into the trees, which seemed to separate with his passing. The dirt path merged with the masses of vegetation, vanishing amongst the wild. The branches ripped at his flesh, thorns eliciting blood offerings, pouring onto the dirt untouched by human hands.

Marco could hear the sound of a flute, resonating either inside his head or in the air. Something short and fuzzy scuttled past his bare feet. Only then did he realize that the only piece of clothing on his body was a pair of light blue boxer shorts. While he walked the branches clawed at his legs. A snag caught the fabric of his shorts and they tore gently off his buttocks. He had been reduced to his most natural form, that which he'd been born into the natural world.

The path sloped upwards. The route seemed familiar, though it wasn't one he'd physically taken. At night it was odd to hear birds chirping singsongly, more pleasant than he'd ever heard them. They seemed almost to be singing *for* him. Finally, the path broke apart, leading to a small clearing where a boulder sat thinking and a small stream bubbled. The strangest feeling came across him when he reached the open expanse, one that begged him to lie down and fall asleep. The Earth looked comfortable.

His body was warm against the damp soil. The sod felt grainy on his back. The stars in the sky were stunning, shining forever, and the moon— oh, the moon. The moon was a ball of wax, cratered and smiling. The scene was like an absurd dream. Yet, unlike his recent dreams he was free to act, free to observe. Marco beheld his body, all bones and shrinking muscle. He had not noticed, but his form was diminishing like Manuel's and his mother's. His ankles were thin and meatless, his calves a weak representation of what they once consisted.

From the tip of his toe, a small snail started to climb across his foot. He didn't brush it off, but stared into its two bulbous eyes. The skin of his chest and arms started to brown in the aftermath of the glorious moon.

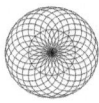

She stood at the window, grimacing. A few strands of wet hair draped over her face. Sometimes she would stand at the window for hours, longing for Marco's return. Though he never came, she held onto hope. Over the long months, Sheila's concern mutated into grief and turned into guilt, regret, and then remorse.

The night he vanished she had called to him, had opened the window and yelled his name over and over, but he simply walked on in a trancelike state, never acknowledging her. It would have been easy to follow him, to pull his arm until he came back to bed. Yet, for some reason—whether she was tired or untroubled—she returned to bed.

Much like the night of his disappearance, it was bleak outside—the trees were swaying, the wind talking, even the birds chirping. The differences rested in the absence of Marco and the absence of the machine.

She never brought it up to anyone, for fear of sounding crazy, but knew Marco had done something miraculous. In the depths of her soul, she just knew he'd gone into the forest with a purpose. Not days beyond, the machines started to sink below the surface. Manuel's breathing reverted to normal. Communications began to slowly, but surely, turn on. She connected with both of her parents (thank God they were alive) and told them the news. They pretended to be sympathetic, but she knew they were deceitful in their condolences. They'd always hated Marco, and death would not force a change.

Conspiracy theories surfaced—from loonies and professionals alike—that the machines were alien weapons, terrorist weapons, or ancient farming tools. Scientists and archaeologists called them the Eighth Wonder of the World. Sheila was ignorant in terms of speculation, but did know that the machines began to disappear on the coattails of Marco's death. She just knew in her heart that Marco had figured a way to save her life.

He had been selfless, dedicated to his family, had done so much for her. She could never possibly repay him. Even if she had a method to do so, Marco was forever gone. She would never again see his smiling face, would never kiss his smooth lips. The only thing Ana and Phillip had found was a pair of his shredded boxers, hanging off of a bush—no blood, no parts, no body. After three months of expeditions, they declared him legally dead. She wished for one more caress of his dark skin.

To keep her company, Marco's mother moved in for good, but it still felt like living alone. She couldn't look at their home the same way. The bed was a constant reminder of his beautiful body, lying there alive and warm. Her one true love, and the one person who'd understood her, would never again step through the door. She could never welcome him home with a hug.

All she had left were the memories. Most of them were great (time spent together holding each other, making jokes, being happy), but there were also memories she wished to bury. She realized that no relationship is ever perfect, but she wanted to remember Marco for his kindness, not his faults. For Sheila, their relationship was ideal. Marco knew exactly what she needed at any given time. Nobody could or would ever replace him. He had sacrificed so much for her (so much for the world!), and the lesson would be ingrained on her brain.

She couldn't understand (and couldn't stomach) how people so effortlessly moved on after the passing of a significant other. To her, it was a task simply to feign poise. They had done almost everything together. They had shared a life. How could she forget and build a new one, as if Marco had never been there? Everywhere she looked was something new to retell his story.

Her eyes wandered past the clearing, where the machine had once spun mercilessly. She hoped they were gone for good, that in her lifetime nothing remotely close to a catastrophe would occur. It was something she *did* want to forget, but also knew it would forever be in the back of her head.

Somewhere in the twilight an owl hooted. She couldn't see the creature, but recognized the hollow voice, calling her attention toward the woodland. Something within the hoot was very charming. She couldn't exactly place the intriguing quality, but it seemed nearly human. She let the blinds slide down, covering the pane of glass in fear of being drawn into the trees like Marco. The forest could be a beautiful, yet sinister, entity.

Sheila eased beneath the comforter, feeling safe and warm in the spot where Marco had slept night after night. She smelled his unwashed pillowcase, searching for a lingering scent which was not present. Lying there, her mind conjured the sound of the constant, dreadful humming that had once been constantly present, the bane of Marco's insomnia. It was joyfully replaced by the incessant hoots of the brilliant owl, cooing her to sleep.

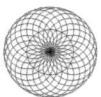